Kaanduri and Other Stories

DASH BENHUR (whose real name is Jitendra Narayan Dash), born in 1953 in Khandapara, a retired Reader in Political Science, is a popular and prolific writer of short stories in Odia. He has been selected for the Bal Sahitya Puraskar, 2014, by the Sahitya Akademi for his contribution to children's literature, of which he is considered Odisha's leading exponent. He started publishing stories for adults as well as children while he was in college, when he adopted his pen-name, inspired by a famous Hollywood film. His rural upbringing moulds his characters who seem caught between memory and desire, village and the city, cynicism and idealism.

BIKRAM KESHARI DAS, born in 1935, a former Professor of English at the Central Institute of English and Foreign Languages, Hyderabad, is a linguist, lexicographer, editor of textbooks, and a translator of Odia fiction and poetry, receiving the first Sahitya Akademi Translation Prize, 1989, which helped to open doors for other translators from Odia. His publications include *Wordmaster Learner's Dictionary of Modern English* and English translations of the works of Odia writers Gopinath Mohanty, Pratibha Ray and Sitakant Mohapatra, winners of the Jnanpith Award, India's highest literary honour.

Kaanduri and Other Stories

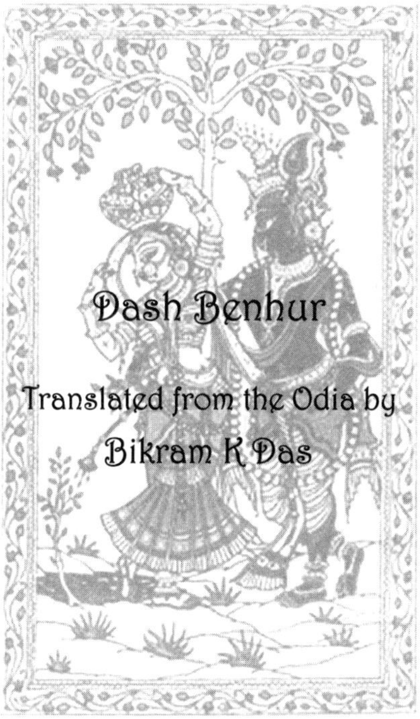

Dash Benhur

Translated from the Odia by

Bikram K Das

Orient BlackSwan

KAANDURI AND OTHER STORIES

ORIENT BLACKSWAN PRIVATE LIMITED

Registered Office
3-6-752 Himayatnagar, Hyderabad 500 029 (Telangana), India
e-mail: centraloffice@orientblackswan.com

Other Offices
Bangalore, Bhopal, Chennai, Ernakulam,
Guwahati, Hyderabad, Jaipur, Kolkata,
Lucknow, Mumbai, New Delhi, Noida, Patna

First Published by Orient Blackswan Pvt. Ltd. 2015

ISBN 978 81 250 5744 4

Sketches by Dr Dinanath Pathy of Bhubaneswar courtesy of the author.

Typeset by
Le Studio Graphique, Gurgaon 122 001
in Sabon LT Std 10/12

Printed at
B. B. Press
Noida

Published by
Orient Blackswan Private Limited
1/24 Asaf Ali Road
New Delhi 110 002
e-mail: delhi@orientblackswan.com

Contents

Illustrations

Preface

Odia, the language spoken by over four crore inhabitants of Odisha, has acquired the official status of a 'classical' Indian language—a distinction hitherto accorded only to Sanskrit and the four Dravidian languages, out of the nearly 1000 languages that exist within our shores. This is an acknowledgement of the fact that Odia has a recorded history and a literary tradition of more than 1500 years and is not derived from any other language. Ironically, about 150 years ago, Odia was about to be removed from the school curriculum, in the land of its own birth, on the ground that it was not an independent language at all but only a debased dialect of Bengali, not deserving a place in education. It was the British civil servant and self-taught linguist, John Beames, who came to its rescue.

History has, on the whole, not been kind to Odisha, despite nature's generosity. Odisha is potentially one of the richest states in the country on account of its mineral and forest wealth, yet it leads all the states (with one possible exception) in poverty and backwardness. The most monumental event in Odisha's entire history, for which it is celebrated, was the humiliating defeat inflicted on it by the Emperor Ashoka. However, the ignominy of defeat brought its own rewards. It was in Odisha that the Buddha found his earliest disciples; it was from this land that the new gospel of peace and non-violence travelled east, south and north to the rest of Asia. After that, history seems to have bypassed Odisha for several centuries: there is little record of Odisha's role in the evolving political narrative, and the region's triumphs and achievements are more the subject of folklore than authenticated history. Fortunately, the temples of Odisha have survived to bear testimony to Odisha's cultural richness, and it was out of these temples that the arts as well as literature of the land grew. Odisha continued to suffer neglect under the Moghul and British administrations, being tagged on to neighbouring Bengal for almost the entire period. Perhaps the most significant events that took place at this time were the series of famines that devastated Odisha. The racial identity, which had almost been lost, took a very long time to be revived; the image of Odisha and Odias that lingered was that of a lethargic race, mired in ignorance, superstition and want. Their language was derided and ridiculed.

The literature that Odisha produced in the nineteenth and early twentieth centuries was born mainly out of suffering. It was the voice of an agrarian and largely feudal society in transition, with traditional patterns of social behaviour and family relationships threatened by the rising tide of individualism, seeking but rarely finding fulfilment, sustained only by its spiritual ballast. One of the pioneers of 'modern' Odia literature was Fakirmohan Senapati, who started his literary career as a poet, turning to fiction in middle age. His story 'Rebati,' the chronicle of a young girl who faces social persecution because of her passion for education, is regarded as the first short story in Odia. Inevitably, Odia fiction was influenced by trends in European, particularly English, Literature, but indigenous traditions of storytelling have continued to engage the Odia imagination. That is why social realism has never entirely dominated the world of Odia fiction: the allegorical mode comes back again and again.

Although a number of Odia writers, notably Manoj Das, Jayanta Mohapatra, J. P. Das, Ramakant Rath, Sitakant Mohapatra and Pratibha Ray, have in recent years won national recognition, other eminent Odia writers remain little known outside their own territory. One reason may be the fact that some of their best work has not yet been translated into English, although translations in other Indian languages are available. The incontrovertible fact remains that English, which still draws conflicting responses from writers and critics in this country, has become the most effective medium for the dissemination of indigenous cultures across language boundaries in India.

This collection of short stories by Dash Benhur is an attempt to bring another writer, well known in Odisha but little read or discussed outside the state, to a wider audience. Dash Benhur has been writing short stories for more than forty years and is also renowned as a columnist. He is best known, however, as a purveyor of *Shishu Sahitya* (Children's Literature)—a genre that few aspiring Odia writers will deign to touch, because once a writer is branded a 'paedio-graphist', catering to juvenile sensibilities, readers as well as critics (a rare species in Odisha) tend to view his/her 'adult' output with condescension. We would like readers of Dash Benhur's stories in translation, who may or may not have read his 'other' work, to judge for themselves just how incisive his insights into the adult's world of Odisha are. We think they will find rather more of the flavour of Odisha in these stories than they would in many other writers, as Dash Benhur, because of his upbringing, is steeped in the culture of hinterland Odisha, which is fast disappearing.

BIKRAM DAS

Glossary of Odia Words

arisha	A kind of fried *pitha* made from wheat or rice flour and molasses. See *pitha*.
bada babu	Head clerk.
balti	Bucket.
bidi	Thin Indian cigarette.
chakki	Millstone used especially by housewives to grind wheat.
chappal	Type of slipper.
chooda	Raw rice dried and pounded flat, used as a snack.
darshan	Among Hindus, 'auspicious sight,' such as a glimpse of a deity in a temple or of a great guru.
dhala	Brass jug without handle.
dhibiri	Kerosene lamp.
ekoisia	Twenty-first day ceremony for a newborn child.
gamuchcha	Towel.
ganji	Vest.
gara	Brass water-pot with a round belly.
go-hatya	Cow slaughter, considered a crime, or sin, among Hindus.
gurudakshina	The Indian tradition of repaying (by monetary or other means) one's teacher or guru after a period of study, as an acknowledgement of respect.
guru maa	The wife of one's guru.
haat	Village market.
holi	The Hindu festival of colours.
jhola	Cloth bag slung from the shoulder.

-ji	Suffix to a name to denote respect.
kacheri	Office or court.
kakara	A kind of *pitha*.
kanta-bilei	Literally, 'a cat with iron claws', a device with hooks to lift articles from, say, the bottom of a well.
katuri	Curved knife.
khadi	Handspun and hand-woven cloth, usually made of cotton.
khai	Popped rice.
lota	Small round metal container for water.
mahaprasad	Cooked food first offered to Jagannath, the foremost deity of Odisha, and then consumed by devotees.
mana	Small wicker basket used to measure out grain, worshipped as a deity during the *mana osha* harvest festival in Margasira (November–December).
manda	A kind of *pitha* with various kinds of fillings, made from steamed rice flour.
moodhi	Raw rice popped in an oven, used as a snack.
mousa	The husband of one's *mausi* (mother's sister). The term is also used to address or refer to any elderly male.
nagra	Open shoes with pointed toes, worn usually by the aristocracy.
nana	Term used, especially in Brahmin families, to address one's father or elder brother.
nanda	Stone ribs (in a well).
nani	Odia equivalent of elder sister.
osha	A festival during which women observe a ritual fast.
paayas	Sort of creamy rice pudding.
pakhala	Cooked rice washed or a little fermented in water.

pitha	Generic name for a range of snacks, sweet or savoury, fried, baked or steamed, prepared especially on festive occasions from various ground cereals and beans.
pranam	Respectful form of greeting of an elder or superior, like namaskar, often involving touching the feet of the person greeted.
pranami	Gift or money offered to someone, especially a teacher or a priest, as a mark of respect.
punjabi	Loose shirt worn by Indian males, resembling a kurta.
purohit	Hindu family priest.
rajo	Seasonal festival celebrated at the start of the sowing operation, representing the earth's menstrual cycle and readiness to receive the seed; young girls celebrate by swinging on *jhoola*s (ropes slung from branches of trees) and singing special festive songs.
saar	The sound of 'sir' as sometimes pronounced by Indians addressing teachers or other elders.
sahukar	Moneylender.
Savitri amavasya	A Hindu festival on a moonless night.
shamiana	Pavilion.
sila	Flat piece of stone used to grind spices into paste for cooking.
sindoor	Vermilion powder applied by married Hindu women to their hair.
tava	Large, flat metal plate used for cooking.
ustad	Honorific title for a highly regarded male teacher or artist, often a musician.
zamindar	Powerful landlord of earlier times.

1. Do Not Come Down, Oh Rain!

She loves the rain. When the rains come, even the sight of an unseasonal berry will make her tingle with excitement; her entire being hums and rings like a dancer's bells. Before the rain's pattering feet have descended, her own feet awaken; tentatively at first, as though drunk with the scattered fragrance. Then, when the raindrops have touched her with sensitive fingertips, her mind gets wrapped in a feeling of ecstasy. If I happen to be at home when a shower begins, she will say, 'Come, let us sit out in the verandah.' The rain may wet her sari to the knees but she will not stir. Sitting beside her, I relish in solitude her communion with the rain. On such a day I ask her, in jest, 'Whom do you love more—me or the rain?' and slyly she replies, 'You—when the rain has drenched you.' To keep that memory alive, I inscribed, below the photograph on the first page of the family album: 'She and I, in the rain.'

She inhabits a different earth when the rains arrive. Everything is drenched in joy, as though the ocean has spread everywhere. She blooms in the all-embracing dance of raindrops. At such a moment, when we two are sitting silently together, I bend towards her and whisper into her ear, as though to tickle her fancy, '*B..a..r..s..h..a*!' (Rain). The murmuring makes her shiver; her eyelids droop.

But how would the rain make her feel today—this untimely rain, in impossible circumstances? She had never experienced this before. Today's rain was unprecedented for her. For the first time, I saw her shrink with apprehension in the middle of that plenitude.

When it rains, she likes to expose herself to it, deliberately. She loves to feel the raindrops splashing down on her face and body. In her childhood, she has told me, she was often scolded by her

Translated from the Odia story 'Barasa Jharana Go,' published in *Navi Samudra*, Agraduta, Cuttack, 1982.

parents for this habit. Her weakness for rain has landed her in many a difficult situation. Once, after she had walked all the way home from school in pouring rain, she caught a severe infection. When she recovered, three weeks later, she was like a dry twig. But she was still unable to resist the sight of rain. Her grandmother had named her 'Barsha-ranka' (rain-addict). She had been unable to give up her addiction even after she came to our family as a bride. If either of my parents was around, in the village or in our home in town, she couldn't indulge in her passion for rain: all she could do then was to stick her head out of a window through which the rain was streaming in. She would remain thus even after she had got soaked. My mother, observing her a couple of times, told her, 'What childishness is this? How can you tell your children not to get wet in the rain when you are like a big child yourself?' She was subdued for a while when she had been ticked off, but soon she was her usual self again. She can't help putting out her hand to greet the rain. They are childhood friends.

But today's rain had frightened her completely. She was recoiling, as though to say, 'Rain, please stop for a moment, won't you? Stop that mad dance! Let us reach our home, and then you can dance as long as you please! We shall be friends again!'

But the rain wouldn't stop. It had started a long time back—long before evening fell. Its frenzy was undiminished. There were brief moments of respite, and then the lightning would spread its wings again across the entire sky. The earth was helpless against that fierce laughter of light. The thunder would come crashing, like mountains tumbling down from the heavens. The skies were heavy with menace.

Who would not be frightened by those thick ropes of rain, those riotous peals of lightning, the roll of thunder? Fear had turned her into a statue. She had become a pale reflection of herself, like an image seen in a cheap mirror.

Suddenly there was another boom of thunder. She shook all over and gripped me in terror, but the next moment her hand slackened and withdrew. In a voice choked with anxiety she said, 'Oh, what shall I do? Why did I ask you to step out of the house when you have such high fever? Shame on me!' I replied, 'Don't worry, the rain will stop soon. We will reach home. Maybe my body feels a little warmer than usual because I've got wet in the rain.' I could sense the fever rising but I was trying to be brave.

A major festival in our village is *mana osha*, which comes to a close on the last Thursday of Margasira (November–December). The women of the house are awake after midnight and start preparing for the puja; the kitchen is filled with baskets of *kakara*, *arisha*, *manda* and other kinds of *pitha*. Early in the morning, the women anoint themselves with turmeric and take a ritual bath—the *kanchan snana* or 'gold bath'—and put on new saris. The house reverberates with festivity. A *mana*, dressed up in a silk sari to represent the goddess Lakshmi, is installed on a little throne and worshipped. The pithas prepared on that day are enjoyed by everyone for the next fortnight. I was so attached to this traditional ceremony that I made it a point to return to our village every year on the last Thursday of Margasira, wherever I might be; after I was married, my wife and I never missed the occasion.

And so it was that the two of us made the 150-kilometre-long journey from my place of work to the village on my motorcycle. We had planned to return on Friday after participating in the ceremonies on Thursday, since my mother would never allow us to leave on a Saturday. The sky was a clear blue when we started; there wasn't a cloud in sight, we had hoped to reach home just as darkness fell. I had proposed that we start early in the morning, as I was a little feverish: perhaps the bath in the village pond hadn't suited me. But my wife said this would make my mother unhappy—so we didn't start until 4.00 in the afternoon. We had gone barely fifteen kilometres when the sky darkened. A chill wind was blowing. 'Is it going to rain?' I asked and my wife, riding pillion, replied, 'Oh, it's going to be all right. You're in the habit of worrying unnecessarily.' She wrapped her arm tighter around my waist and I smiled.

But the black clouds grew. Folk wisdom says the clouds of Margasira are rainless, but these must have been exceptional.

A lonely village road. On either side were numerous square pits, out of which basketfuls of earth had been excavated and laid on the road surface. The wind blew unfettered across the fields. Would it grow into a storm? The thought was unnerving. I tightened my grip on the throttle of the motorcycle. We were racing through clouds of red dust. Two human beings sick with apprehension—and soon, two human beings soaked in the rain. Raindrops as big as plums beat down mercilessly. Looking around desperately for shelter I saw, at a little distance, a clump of mango trees underneath one of which was a tiny hut. Leaving the motorcycle on the road we ran to the hut. It had no door, and the roof, made of palm fronds, was gaping. Not much of a shelter but still ...

As the rain showed no signs of abating, I thought it unwise to leave the motorcycle in the open; water might get into the engine. I ran out into the lashing rain and started to walk back, trundling the bike along. The wheels were sinking in the soft mud and I wasn't making much progress. I had to leave it in the open once again and hurry back. I was shivering now.

The two of us trapped in that hut, helpless; outside, the unrelenting rain, as unforgiving as the tirade of a near relative after a misunderstanding. When would it end? It was growing dark.

How we could have enjoyed the rain if we had been in the safety of our own home! But alas, the treacherous circumstances! What could my wife be thinking? That her beloved rain had turned into a curse? If it had been some other time and place, I would surely have teased her and had some fun at her expense.

She always hated the dark. One night in the village, soon after we were married, she needed to go to the bathroom. 'What a strange house this is!' she had exclaimed aloud. 'The bathroom is in the backyard!' I guessed she wanted me to accompany her and got up. It had been drizzling, but suddenly there was a peal of thunder. 'Oh, mother!' she screamed, and ran to me and held me tight. It had taken just one thunderbolt to blow away all her pride. I was grateful to the rain!

But tonight it was different. There was no way I could enjoy the effect of the rain on her. I could only hope it would take pity on us and stop.

We were crouching in one corner of the hut, trying to shield ourselves from the downpour. She was almost in tears after she became aware of my fever. The wind rushed in through the open doorway, accompanied by sheets of rain. 'We must close this door somehow,' I said, shivering with fever. It was pitch-dark outside. Then suddenly, the lightning flashed, and I saw her clothed only in her undergarments. She had taken off her sari and hung it across the doorway. 'Oh rain!' she cried, tears streaming down her face. 'Stop, for God's sake!'

I can't remember how the night ended, but undoubtedly it did, for here we are, together, looking at the photograph in our album. 'She and I in the rain!' But we carry another memory, another experience of the rain.

2. The Apartment

'Hello! Hello! HELLO!'

I woke up with a start.

Who could it be? Sounded like an elderly person. But should he be shouting so loudly over the telephone, this early in the morning? Weren't the neighbours entitled to a little peace?

An apartment in a new block of apartments. The bedroom of one was a mere six feet away from the balcony of the next. True, you couldn't see the balcony, but the sound was still echoing like an explosion. If you were woken up once it was difficult to go back to sleep. It was 2.00 a.m. by my watch when I had finished all my chores and gone to sleep. My eyes were still burning. I could have had another two hours of sleep. My wife and daughter were asleep in the other room; obviously, the sound hadn't reached them.

I tried and tried but sleep wouldn't come. The 'hello! hello!' had gone on and I had been obliged to get up.

I went through my morning ablutions in a state of great irritation. Another three hours to go before I could start for the office. My wife and daughter were still sleeping; they had gone to bed late, tired after the exertion of unpacking and arranging things.

'Swapna Apartments' it was called. Initially, I had misread the name as 'Swapn Apartments'—the Dream House, the correct name being merely its feminine version, so to speak. Soundly constructed with an attractive finish. A modern eight-storeyed apartment block surrounded by a cluster of similar buildings. Expensive. All the occupants, whether tenants or owners, were well-to-do and sophisticated. Thirty-two apartments to a block—one hundred and

Translated from the Odia story 'Apartment,' published in *Taraluthiba Samaya*, Bharata Bharati, Cuttack, 2010.

twenty-eight in all. If each apartment sheltered four persons, there would be more than five hundred souls in that vertical village. But as it was a city within a city, all were busy with their own affairs. No one felt obliged to know one's neighbours. Who had the time anyway?

My wife and I had liked the place immediately. She liked the surroundings and I the isolation. There were so many living there but you couldn't hear a sound. The rent was high, more than my employer would allow, but I was attracted by the quiet. If you shut the front door, you could enjoy your dreams in peace.

It was far from the heart of the city but the builder had ensured that all modern conveniences were at hand. We had entered the apartment happily only the day before. Last night should have been the beginning of our new dreams but everything had been ruined. If one didn't get sleep, where would the dreams come from? Damn that old neighbour, whoever he was!

But then I thought, why should I allow the thoughtlessness of some unknown person to spoil my tomorrows? I calmed my mind and sat down in front of my computer.

My wife got up and then my daughter.

My wife made me a cup of tea and settled down to life in the kitchen. My daughter got ready to go to her college and I prepared for the office.

There were no problems now. The 'hello, hello' had stopped. I didn't think it necessary to tell my wife what had happened.

I left for the office. It was evening when I returned. My wife gave me a piece of good news as soon as I arrived. 'Do you know,' she said, 'there's a Ganesh temple in the ground floor of this block?' As my wife was addicted to temple-going, this was good news indeed for her, but I found no cause for rejoicing. Instead, I made a little joke and said, 'Wonderful! So we will have the gods under our feet!'

That night I slept well. The bedroom window opened to the south and I could see tall trees in the distance, and beyond them, the dark blue outline of a line of hills. Airplanes coming in to land had to fly low over them. In short, the view from my new home was perfect! Living in a tower block of apartments was like living in the sky! The foot of the tower was the appropriate place for both gods and motor cars. Temples and garages have a natural affinity for each other, for it is the gods who give you passage to the realms above, sending you on a high-speed journey in a celestial car.

'Hello! Hello! Hello!'

That harsh, ear-splitting sound again. After two days of peace the rusty voice was back, at the very same spot, with the very same intensity! My sleep was shattered again, early in the morning.

I tried to control myself, thinking of Gandhiji. 'The wise man turns all disadvantages into advantages,' he had said. Well, good! Since I was awake, I could go back to Amartya Sen's *The Argumentative Indian* which I had begun reading three days earlier.

The next two days passed without incident—but it was too good to last. 'Hello, hello, hello!' again—the same voice, as loud and piercing as ever.

It was too much. My inner being mutinied. I shook my wife awake. Poor thing—she had been in deep slumber: 'Get me a cup of tea with some ginger!' She muttered, only half awake, 'I have a bad headache!' I could have managed the tea myself, but I had woken her up because I needed someone to share my woes. As we sipped tea, I presented my list of allegations against the old neighbour. 'After I leave for the office, can you find out who our neighbour in Number 412 is? And why he feels compelled to come out and stand in the balcony, outside my bedroom window, every other day, and shout "Hello, hello," early in the morning?' I said to my wife.

There was a reason for my delegating this responsibility to her. She is much more level-headed than I am and more adept at negotiating delicate social situations. Whenever I attempted it, the effect was invariably disastrous. She had told me so herself. So I left for the office, confident that the affair would be managed effectively.

When I returned that evening the investigation was complete. 'Number 412 is occupied by a gentleman of about seventy-five who lives alone, does his own cooking and scarcely ever goes out. If he needs anything, he has it brought up by the security people downstairs. His son and daughter-in-law are in America, daughter and son-in-law in Switzerland. His wife passed away ten years back. No relatives or friends ever visit him. He was in government service years ago and after having wandered over various parts of the state, it's been five years since he decided to buy this apartment in the state capital so that his children will have a place to stay when they come to India.'

'Thanks for the résumé,' I said. 'But why the shouting outside my window? Didn't you ask?'

'Is that a question one can ask directly?' she replied. 'After all, he is old. He must have problems which you wouldn't be able to understand. He could be hard of hearing, you know.'

'Yes, but surely he can find some other place in a 1200-square foot apartment to exercise his vocal cords? Is the balcony the only space available? And why do you have to plead on his behalf?'

She didn't reply and I decided to drop the matter.

The night was uneventful. But it started again the very next morning. 'Hello ... hello ... hello!'

I woke up, burning with annoyance. I didn't feel like reading or browsing the Net and neither the cup of tea nor the newspaper could interest me. After tossing in bed for some time I got up and went through my morning routine, then got dressed for the office.

My wife woke up at the usual time, saw me dressed and asked, surprised, 'Where are you going so early?'

'To the office,' I said briefly.

'But you didn't tell me you would be leaving this early,' she complained, and stepped into the kitchen, where she would spend much of the rest of the day.

I went down to the ground floor and got into the lift on the other side. Number 412 had its front door facing the other way, although it was next to ours.

I stood in front of the door and rang the bell. The name-plate above the bell said 'Abhinay Sharan Mohanty, Retired Chief Engineer.' The elderly gentleman opened the door, coughing slightly. Thin, wispy hair. A ladle in his hand—he had obviously been cooking. He didn't look pleased to see me.

Feeling a little flustered, I stammered, 'Sir, I am your neighbour in 407. My name is Dharmanand—Dharmanand Das.'

'I am busy now,' he said in a voice devoid of emotion. 'Could you come back in the evening?'

What could I have said? There were ripples of anger coursing through my body. 'Too busy to talk to me,' I said to myself, ' but not too busy to disturb my sleep at 4.00 in the morning. Some gentleman!'

Without uttering a word I raised my hands in a namaskar and walked away. I had barely turned my back when the door slammed shut with a bang.

Straight to the office I went and busied myself in work. But somehow, the elderly gentleman's long face and those straw-like wisps of hair wouldn't leave me alone. 'Hello ... hello ... hello' I could hear, as though someone was mocking me.

I deliberately left the office early. But instead of returning to my own apartment I went directly to No. 412.

The door opened as soon as I rang the bell. The elderly gentleman emerged, with a wide smile on his face, and practically dragged me by the hand into his apartment—such was the effusiveness of his welcome. 'You're back?' he asked. 'Must have come directly from the office. I've just made some tea for myself; come, we'll have it together.'

I noticed that the apartment was full of expensive objects. But they had been arranged haphazardly and were thickly coated with dust.

The gentleman returned from the kitchen with two cups of tea on a tray. 'What did you say your name was?' he asked, as he sat down. 'Oh yes, Dharmanand, isn't it? Tell me, Dharmanand Babu, what was it you wanted to see me about?'

I was speechless. All my anger and irritation had evaporated. Poor old man, I thought. How much wealth he must have accumulated; in what luxury he must have brought up his children! With a host of minions to fulfil every wish! But now—all alone. Completely alone. Even the expensive frame of his glasses was filthy with grime. Crumpled shirt on top of an unwashed lungi. Years of loneliness imprinted on his face. What complaint could I make?

All I could say was, 'Sir, I am your new neighbour in 407. I moved in about a fortnight ago. I hear you talking on the phone every morning and thought I'd come and meet you. I am the Assistant Manager in the Ferguson Company. I have one daughter; she's in college.'

The gentleman made no attempt to find out anything about me. Did not offer to visit my apartment. Didn't ask me to bring my wife and daughter on my next visit.

All he said was that his son and daughter lived abroad. 'I have to get up early if I want to ring them up,' he said. 'The signal from the telecom tower isn't very good inside this apartment. It's much better on the other balcony, though, and that's where I go when I want to talk to them. But the connection is frequently disrupted. I'm sure you can hear me!'

The face which had borne a smile a moment ago suddenly underwent a change—like a *pitha* which had been turned over on the *tava*. The side which I could see now looked singed and blackened.

'Sir, allow me to take leave of you now,' I said and got up to go.

When I reached my apartment I said to my wife, 'I visited our "Hello, hello" neighbour just now. The balcony on our side is where he makes his phone calls because that's where the signal is good. You know what that means, don't you? We'll have to leave this apartment.'

My wife didn't react at all.

Later, when the three of us were having dinner, she said, 'Both Rupa's college and your office are quite close to this place. And if you do move to another place, can you be sure it will be quieter than this? What if the neighbour's daughter is taking dance lessons or their son likes loud music? Will you go and fight with them? Rupa and I will move your bed to the other bedroom. You can shift there.'

I had nothing to say to them. On the contrary, my daughter said, 'Father, remember, the other name for staying in an "apartment" is "adjustment."'

Did I need this lesson from anyone?

3. Arrogance

There was sadness in the air as people spoke of Chhota (a man of small build, who happened to be lame). But Satura seemed to have turned into a block of stone; neither tears nor words were left in him.

One of Chhota's legs had been stunted by polio. From the chest to the waist he was as compact as a sandbag. Long wavy locks on his head, two front teeth missing, and a shiny, jet black body, a nose as blunt and rounded as a snail, and a rasping voice in which he trumpeted out his call-sign: 'Any *dhala*s, *gara*s, *balti*s to be taken out of your wells?'

He must have been past forty. Lame though he was, his vitality was amazing. No one knew what his real name was: he was 'Chhota' to nearly thirty villages in the vicinity.

He appeared for just a day or two each year in any village.

Blistering heat that would turn a fistful of ripe paddy into *khai* in a moment if you scattered it on the stones at the entrance to the village. People hid from the sun behind closed doors and windows. That was when Chhota would appear. Bare feet, bare head. Rivers of sweat running down his body. A hand-woven five-yard Khordha *gamuchcha* round his hips, with the folds tucked in tightly; another gamuchcha wrapped around his waist like a cummerbund. On one shoulder he carried a coil of rope. As soon as he reached the village his cry rang out: 'Dhalas, garas, baltis to take out?' It was a unique cry. Not designed to attract or to search. Flat and toneless. Although it was meant to announce his presence there was an arrogance concealed in the cry—a kind of defiance. More a battle cry than an announcement.

Translated from the Odia story 'Bahapa,' published in *Taraluthiba Samaya*, Bharata Bharati, Cuttack, 2010.

There were sixty-two houses in Ratankud village but only about thirteen or fourteen wells. Tima Ratha's narrow well was reinforced with *nanda*s. The Padhana family's well was deep, with a wide mouth; on a block of marble, at a place where every user of the well was bound to leave footprints, the Padhanas had inscribed the names of their departed parents. The others werc just ordinary wells. But one well, which was in a thicket where hornbills nested, at some distance from the village, and had been dedicated to the goddess Piteisuni, was strange. Not strange so much as fearsome. It had been dug out of solid rock. Wide at the mouth, but the deeper you went the narrower it seemed to become. No one knew just how deep it was. Naba Taonla, the head of the Saora village whose patron goddess Piteisuni was, told someone that he had once tied two coils of thick rope end to end and lowered them into the well to find out how deep it was, but the end of the rope never touched bottom. The water was sweet and crystal clear. But a thick clump of weeds and bushes had grown out of the stone walls just a few feet below the mouth and practically choked the well. Someone had laid the trunk of a thick *sal* tree across the open mouth of the well and people stood on it as they drew water from the well.

Whenever there was a festival or a ritual puja to Piteisuni, people assembled in large numbers near the well but at other times it was deserted.

It was wells that took Chhota from one village to another. During the rainy season, the wells were overflowing and the level did not recede much in winter. But every summer the wells dried up. The well in Sapaneswar village, on the other side of Ratankud, went so dry that you could see the bottom. People drew water in *lota*s, garas and buckets which they lowered into the wells with a rope knotted or looped around their mouths and inevitably some slipped out and fell to the bottom. Who would dare to take them out of the deep wells? Tima Ratha owned a *kanta-bilei*, a metal device fitted with long curved hooks meant for just this purpose, but he never lent it to anyone. If a neighbour asked him for it he would come up with a dozen excuses; his wife would say, in her nasal voice, 'I don't know where it is. Someone must have put it in the attic upstairs.' The kanta-bilei was a most useful contraption—you tied it to a rope and lowered it to the bottom of the well and trawled it around; any pots, mugs or other vessels that happened to be lying there would be caught in the protruding claws, like fish-hooks, and you only had to pull it—and them—up slowly.

But the kanta-bilei wasn't always effective. There were times when someone carelessly allowed a brass tumbler or bowl to fall in and then the kanta-bilei was of no use at all. That was why people always waited anxiously for Chhota's coming.

When Chhota came he would sweep the bottom of the well and bring up even the smallest object that someone had let drop—so much so that he had brought up necklaces, rings and bangles. Sometimes he had to go down three or four times in quest of something that had sunk into the thick mud at the bottom. The people standing around the well would stare down open-mouthed as Chhota rose like a water-god, announcing, 'Here you are; take it! See how it has been blackened by lying in the mud?'

Many were roused from sleep by Chhota's call. Somewhere a girl would sit up hurriedly and say, 'Mother, mother! Chhota has come!' And the mother would give vent to her relief, speaking of a neighbour, 'Her gara has been lying in the well for seven or eight months now; who was there to bring it out? Poor girl—what abuse she has had to suffer since the gara fell into the well! First, it was her mother-in-law who took her to task, then her sister-in-law and finally her husband refused to talk to her! That's why daughters-in-law in this village are so excited when Chhota is here! Everyone has something lying at the bottom of a well.'

If elders were anxious to recover what they had lost, youngsters were equally keen to see the feats that Chhota performed.

Whoever called out to Chhota first on his arrival had prior claim on his services. The villagers would congregate in the backyard and Chhota's boasting would begin. 'That well in the next village! Who knows how deep that *saala** is! Must be fifty hands at least. The water is like ice! And the mud—waist deep! But I'm not one to let the saala go! I raked up the mud from top to bottom. Two lotas, three garas and four buckets I pulled out! God knows how long one of the buckets had lain there; the saala's bottom was hanging out!'

The villagers gaped. Children stared in disbelief. Even the young men were impressed.

* Terms of abuse like '*saala*' (literally, wife's brother, i.e., brother-in-law) are used even for lifeless objects and sometimes among friends in colloquial speech.

But once Satura asked him, 'Can you bring up a gold ring from a well?'

Chhota paused for a moment. Then he said, 'It's difficult—but it can be done. One would have to get inside the mud three or four times and grope around. But the cost will be much higher for such work—I must tell you that.'

It was mere talk but the students of the high school who lived in the village didn't like it. They said to each other when he was not around, 'The smart alec likes to boast when he comes to our village. What does he take us for? Can anyone stand in waist-deep mud and bring up a gold ring?"

It was Satura who grumbled the loudest.

The people in all the villages were very fond of Chhota. What a serviceable person he was! If he wasn't there who would bring up all those lost things? When a brass lota or gara falls into a well it's like a heavy rock falling on a poor villager's chest! For them, Chhota is like an angel! 'Let him boast a little if he wants to; how does it harm anybody?' is what the common people thought.

But the young men of the village could not digest his boasting.

When something had to be brought up from someone's well Chhota would first appear at his door, then walk to the foot of the well. He would rub at least half a bottle of sesame oil or castor oil all over his head and body. He tilted his head and put a couple of drops of oil into each ear. The gamuchcha was tucked in a little more tightly between his thighs and then he would call for a *chakki* or a *sila*. He would lift the heavy stone onto his shoulder and limp—but with head proudly erect—to the well. On reaching the well he would put the stone on the ground and tie one end of the rope which lay coiled on his shoulder around it. Then, standing on the log of wood which lay across the mouth of the well, he would release the stone from his hands and let it drop to the bottom. The other end of the rope was tied firmly around the log of wood and now Chhota would grip the rope in both hands and slide down the rope in a flash. When the water was chest high, he would stop and draw in a dozen or so deep breaths and then plunge to the bottom. The oil on his body made the water glisten. The spectators looked down in wonder; one or two complained: 'This water won't be fit to drink for at least a week!' But most paid no attention; everyone was looking at the shaking log of wood lying across the well and the rope that hung from it.

From time to time the rope shook violently. Then suddenly they heard a hissing sound and Chhota's head emerged from the water as he let out a long breath. In his hands there might be a lota or some other vessel. The lost objects were restored to their owners.

It was a wonderful sight. The eyes of the person who received the object shone brightly and Chhota's eyes glistened too with the glow of success.

Chhota returned thus to Ratankud each year, and each time people witnessed his feats. The young men talked about him.

Summer returned and one day Chhota was back too. The familiar call rang out: 'Dhalas, garas, baltis to take out?' Chhota went down into several wells and performed his tasks. It was almost four in the afternoon and he was about to return when Satura came running and said, 'My ring has fallen into the well. Can you bring it out?"

There were three others with Satura. Gopal, Makara and Duruja. Chhota looked at them and said, 'It's almost evening. I'll do it tomorrow. But I tell you—if it's a gold ring I'll take fifty rupees.'

Satura's father was the village *sahukar*. Fifty rupees was no big deal for him. They agreed: Chhota would return the next day and bring out the ring.

He didn't need to ask which well it was that the ring had fallen into. He strode out towards the road proudly like a hero.

When he was back the next day Satura and his friends met him outside the village. Satura said, 'My ring fell into Piteisuni's well. We had gone there for a picnic. The ring slipped out while I was drawing water.'

Chhota looked at him with disbelief in his eyes, and then said, 'Very well, let us go.'

A large, heavy stone was found. There was an old sal log across the well. Chhota tied the stone with a long piece of rope and lowered it into the well. It touched bottom just as it was reaching its end. He tied the upper end to the log, just at its centre.

Satura carried a bottle of oil in his pocket. In his hand he held a *katuri*. 'Good thing you brought the katuri,' said Chhota. He rubbed the oil on his head and body, took the katuri from Satura and tucked it into his waistband.

'Why do you rub all that oil on yourself, Chhota Bhai?' Duruja asked him, and Chhota said, '*Arre*, there are so many kinds of wells

I have to get into. Are all the saalas the same? The cold in the water could get me!"

Now Chhota walked along the log of sal to its middle and slid a little way down the rope. He pulled out the katuri and hacked away the bushes which grew inside the well and returned the katuri to Satura. Then he continued to slide down. His body touched water. He halted, took a deep breath and went in with a splash. Satura and his friends looked down. The wooden log shook; the rope was convulsed.

Long minutes later, Chhota rose to the surface. 'There isn't much mud here,' his voice echoed out of the well, 'but I haven't found it yet. I'll have to go down again.' He went down three times in all.

When he went down the second time, Satura grinned and said, 'Which ring is the saala going to find? There's no ring down there at all! He won't find any ring and I won't give him that fifty rupees.'

The others knew now that Satura had lied. Gopal said, 'That was not a nice thing to do, Satura! Why have you made him do all that work in vain?'

'Why was he boasting to us then?' Satura retorted.

Makara said, 'Why didn't you really drop the ring in? Then we would have seen if he could bring it up!'

Satura became a little subdued.

Just then Chhota rose and went down again into the water. Gopal was about to shout out, 'Come up, Chhota Bhai! There's no ring!'

But before anyone could speak, Chhota had taken several long breaths and gone in again.

By now, they were all feeling dejected. Satura seemed to have realised his mistake. The others were thinking, 'We will beg Chhota's forgiveness when he comes up!'

'Is this what educated boys like us should do?' Gopal said.

All four were staring into the water. All four were thinking to themselves, 'Come up quickly, Chhota Bhai, and forgive us!'

But Chhota seemed to be taking a long time to come up again.

The boys looked at the rope. Looked at the log of wood. Everything looked all right. Almost an hour passed. Chhota did not come up.

The four friends looked at each other and burst into tears.

The people in the village heard what had happened. They gathered round the well. Amid all the shouting and confusion another three or four ropes were lowered into the well. After a lot of effort, Chhota's lifeless body was fished out. Still glistening with oil. The same arrogant look on the face.

'Could be snakebite,' someone said. 'No, no, his lungs must have burst!' said another. Those who were better informed said, 'Heart failure!'

Satura, Gopal, Makura and Duruja stood hanging their heads in remorse.

Then someone said, 'Look, his right fist is clenched tightly. Open it!'

Chhota's closed fist was opened. In it, wrapped in layers of mud, lay a gold ring.

4. The Blankets Are Really Warm!

Having spoken, Charan Babu resumed his mauling of the paan between his jaws, completely at peace with the world.

Smugness wrapped him like a blanket. Where were the deeply-felt words, the impassioned arguments, the cascade of venom, the accusations of incompetence poured out upon the bureaucracy?

That one remark of his made me feel as though a swarm of red ants had suddenly invaded every limb of mine.

How strange it was! Could the same mouth sing such different tunes? Only a week ago he had been seething with anger, punctuating every sentence with obscenities. Standing in the club verandah, he had declared that none of this would be tolerated—he would go on fast in front of the Chief Minister's residence; he would write to everyone, from the Prime Minister to the Chief Justice of India; he would expose everyone in the national papers.

I was aware of Charan Babu's weakness for expensive liquor. He could easily exceed limits when the right brew was inside him but that day he hadn't touched a drop. When discussion had broken out at the club, his had been the most substantial arguments. I could have sworn, therefore, that no beverage was accountable for what he said.

But today's one-line remark had wiped out the uprightness and honesty of earlier days.

He moved his leg up and down slowly, completely relaxed, as he munched paan, without a trace of anxiety or excitement. In the light filtering in through the window, one side of his face appeared, in profile, like that of some animal.

Translated from the Odia story 'Kambala Bhari Garam,' published in *Taraluthiba Samaya*, Bharata Bharati, Cuttack, 2010.

Charan Babu was a renowned journalist, well known among editors as well as readers for his penetrating and objective analyses. His pen could whisper, rage, turn abusive, threaten or cajole as required. He was adept at turning the searchlight on the dark shadows that linger in cracks. His language could be just as gripping as the emotions were stirring. As an admirer, I had often sought his company at the club.

FIGURE 1. 'THOSE SWEDISH BLANKETS ARE REALLY WARM.'

What a hoard of information he possessed!—how many plots of land had been allotted to bureaucrats under various aliases; how many criminals and business sharks were being nursed by political leaders, ... he had all the details. Everyone in the secretariat, from the lift operator to the *bada babu* in the Chief Secretary's office, was his confidant. He could tap his informants without having to stir out of home—but the means he employed were known only to God. You had to give him credit though. Just as wildlife experts can tranquilise dangerous beasts, implant transmitters in their bodies and obtain all kinds of data, he could pry secrets out of babus using some unknown magic. His reports were always supported, therefore, by authentic facts and figures.

What, then, could explain this latest behaviour?

Floods and droughts are commonplace in Odisha and begging for relief is almost the birthright of all Odias. The funds that are received benefit the little cogs in the administrative machine rather than those who have been affected. Charan Babu maintained, therefore: 'The homes and bank accounts of all bureaucrats should be scrutinised after each season of flood or drought!'

After the Great Cyclone that year the condition of Odisha was really pitiable. The situation was so critical that relief poured into the state unsolicited, by land, sea and air. Ersama might have been the epicentre but the entire state had been numbed by a single blow. Lakhs were made homeless; thousands of corpses were strewn across the land. No one knew how many had died and how many made destitute; and who could keep count of the cattle, sheep and goats or trees that had been washed away? The water had turned poisonous; previously-fertile land had acquired a thick deposit of salt. Winter became a torture. Hillocks of dead bodies; row upon row of lifeless homes; thousands of coconut trees with their tops sheared off. Fear spread through the land—even the softest breath of wind or the murmur of flowing water created panic.

But the earth still survived. Odisha recovered with the aid it received. Helping hands were extended, unasked, across the seas. How many organisations and individuals, from countless lands, rushed in to help! Food grains, medicines and clothing arrived in heaps. Some offered to re-build homes; others comforted those who had lost their kin. Succour took a hundred forms.

But many unwanted events happened too. For many, the doors of fortune had suddenly opened. Who could have kept track of all the relief materials that poured in? Items were pilfered while still on the way; trucks were waylaid and even the well-to-do joined the looting. Village sarpanchs who were supposed to direct relief diverted truckloads and boatloads to their own homes; those who had already received aid claimed to have been bypassed and began a reign of terror. It was too good an opportunity to be missed by the distributors of relief. Someone's misfortune became another person's bounty. Human character underwent a change; traditions were swept away. Stretching out hands to beg became a part of dharma.

On just such a day did Charan Babu let out his scream of outrage in the Capital Club. 'Who can save this state now? If our political leaders and top officials set such an example, whom will the ordinary people emulate? Can anyone who has known prosperity rob the beggar's bowl? Will a *zamindar* steal the stale gruel from his farm-labourer's bowl of *pakhala*? But this is exactly what is happening now in Odisha. This is not to be tolerated! I will oppose it strongly.'

What led to this outburst was the fact that the Swedish government had flown in two thousand kits of relief material to help cyclone victims. Each kit contained a miniature polythene tent of advanced design, two expensive blankets, warm baggy trousers and a jacket, undergarments, first-aid equipment, a box of medicines, a flashlight, special nutritive biscuits to ward off starvation, tools for everyday use and a transistor radio. By Western standards, these might have been bare necessities for survival but for Odisha, in the circumstances then prevailing, these were unbelievable treasures. There was a stampede for the Swedish goods.

The news reached Charan Babu. Who could control him now? His shouting could be heard a mile away. His roaring filled the dining room at the club.

I was so affected by Charan Babu's righteous rage that I began to think of what *I* could do to correct the situation. My mind was filled with disgust for the mighty and powerful. I decided to write in the newspapers. I would help in ripping the masks off.

Seven days had passed. That morning, I don't know why, I rushed off to Charan Babu's residence as soon as I had got out of bed and drunk my cup of tea, shivering in the biting winter wind. The sun seemed reluctant to appear. Charan Babu was seated in his drawing room when I reached his house. He smiled faintly on seeing me. After the exchange of salutations, I started talking of the cyclone and everything that had followed.

Charan Babu looked relaxed. Before I could utter anything more, he brought a smile to his broad paan-stained lips and told me, 'Say what you like, Jitu Babu, but those Swedish blankets are really warm! They don't let you feel the winter at all.'

I was startled. But he was clearly beyond the cyclone's reach.

5. The Book Review

A person I know spends so much of his time in trying to obtain favours from people with influence that his hands are now permanently joined in supplication and his voice has developed a peculiar cringing quality, because of which I have named him 'Kakustha Babu,' which is loosely translated as 'Mr Pitiful.' I shall refer to him here, however, merely as 'Babu.'

A new collection of short stories by Babu appeared recently. He is a fairly well-known writer in Odia, having produced eight to ten books. His work appears regularly in magazines and newspapers and he has, in the past, received numerous letters praising his writing, apart from several literary awards and scrolls of honour. It would be correct to say, therefore, that he is a writer with a reputation.

Babu believes, however, that unless the author of a new book can prevail upon friends and acquaintances to write reviews, the world will take no notice of it at all. Like a wild jasmine blossoming unseen in some unknown wilderness, it will wither away. But *where* the review appears is important, since literary journals in Odia are not widely circulated. Moreover, editors have a habit of tucking away reviews in obscure corners of their publications, just as invitations to funerals, delivered by village barbers, are tucked away in the thatch by their recipients and forgotten, since they are considered inauspicious; even if seen, they are seldom read. Hence, the literary page in a daily newspaper is a more suitable place for reviews than literary journals because they are far more widely circulated, and read by all, from kings to beggars. The likelihood of the review being noticed is therefore greater, and so Babu invited to

Translated from the Odia story 'Bahi Samikshya,' published in *Taraluthiba Samaya*, Bharata Bharati, Cuttack, 2010.

his home a journalist working for a prominent newspaper whom he knew well and gave him two copies of his book, requesting him to ensure that a review was published.

Readers may ask—why *two* copies, when one would suffice? Because if you want a book to be reviewed, always give out two copies—one for the organisation that publishes the review and the other for the reviewer.

Be that as it may, Babu discovered suddenly one day, after four months of breathless waiting, that a review *had* appeared—though in an attenuated form. It was more an acknowledgement of 'Books Received' than a review—no bigger in size than the glass phials in which homeopathic medicines are sold. The taste in Babu's mouth turned sour when he saw the review. But what could he say?

FIGURE 2. A BOOK REVIEW NO BIGGER IN SIZE THAN THE GLASS PHIALS IN WHICH HOMEOPATHIC MEDICINES ARE SOLD.

After some time had passed, he met his journalist friend on the street one day. 'What is this you have done?' Babu asked in an accusing tone. 'Such a tiny review? It would have been better not to publish it at all!'

The journalist friend was used to such assaults. He replied, 'No, no, there is some misunderstanding. Let me explain—and then you can decide whether an injustice has been done to you.' Babu had expected some expression of regret, if not an apology. But the journalist friend said, 'You are a famous writer. It is enough just to inform readers that a new book written by you has appeared. When a famous film star makes an appearance in the city, does anyone send out invitations? It's enough to let people know that she has arrived. Believe me, this is a similar situation! Rest assured, sir—we have done just what was needed in your case.'

The words were like an ointment for Babu's injured pride. 'Please don't mind what I said,' he said to the journalist friend. 'It was just a casual remark.'

More days passed. One day, while turning over the pages of the same newspaper, Babu came across the review of a new novel. It ran to considerable length—almost half a page. In the centre was a colour photograph of the book and, below it, that of the author; the reviewer had written lovingly and eloquently about both.

'Who is this writer?' Babu said to himself. 'I don't remember having heard of him before.' In his own case, if not his photograph or a review of the book, at least a picture of the book could have appeared. The journalist was such an intimate friend of his: couldn't he have made sure of this?

He called up his friend at once and asked, 'About this book review that has just appeared—can you tell me who this writer is? None of us know anything about him. Your paper has published his photograph and that of his book, but on the other hand ...'

Before he could complete his sentence the reply came, 'You have misunderstood us again! The author of this book is a newcomer, not known to most readers. That's why the photographs were necessary. But not for a well-known writer such as yourself.'

But Babu did not feel consoled. As an author, *he* might have been well known, but not his book. Couldn't the journalist have published a picture of its cover? Anyway, it was *something* that he had been referred to as a famous writer.

On another day, Babu was sitting in his verandah with the newspaper in his hand. As soon as he turned the page his eyes fell on the review of a new book by a well-known writer, a contemporary of his, highly respected and honoured in literary circles. It was an exhaustive review written in an effusive style. There was a photograph of the author, smiling faintly, along with that of the book.

Now *this* was a well-known author, Babu thought. Then where was the need for that large photograph of the author and his book? And why wasn't it done for *his* book? Of what use was his intimacy with the journalist?

He felt depressed when he saw the review. No, no—there had to be some other explanation. He was being deliberately ignored. So this was what his very good friend was doing! He set off for the newspaper office to find out the truth.

He ran into the journalist friend almost at once. Babu said directly, 'Today's paper carries a long review along with photographs. But this writer is already well known. Therefore, by your own criteria, such a long review should not have been necessary. Readers know him very well already, don't they?'

He was going to bring up the matter of his own book, but the journalist friend anticipated this. He laughed and said, 'You have answered your own question. Readers know him very well. My dear sir, there is a difference between being well known and *very* well known. This writer falls in the latter category. If we had published only a "Books Received" notice for his new publication, readers would have taken us to task. Besides, this would have been a grave injustice to Odia literature.'

Kakustha Babu was rendered speechless. He felt lost in the maze of 'unknown author,' 'well-known author' and '*very* well-known author.' He was merely well known, and so his book merited only a brief review. Judgement had been passed!

No one knew of the wound that had been inflicted on him.

6. Clouds

'I don't like this habit of yours at all,' Sujata said gruffly. 'Did you *have to* show off your generosity? You know I'm diabetic; I need to have some food at short intervals. Those biscuits were all we had and you gave them away to the child! What am I going to eat now? Nothing will be available until we reach Bhubaneswar.'

She turned her face away and sat sulking, her eyes wet.

The Raipur–Bhubaneswar Express chugged along. Sukanta felt uncomfortable. What could he say to her? It was true; all their food was gone. They had started from Raipur at 5.00 last evening. For dinner they had had the food which they had brought with them. The train should have reached Bhubaneswar at 8.00 in the morning but some unknown problem had held them up at Kantabanjhi for three hours, so that it was half past seven when they reached Dhenkanal. Time for Sujata's tea and biscuits.

Ever since she had developed diabetes Sujata was unable to withstand hunger. If she didn't get something to eat at once she became irritable. He had bought a packet of Cream Cracker biscuits for such a contingency, but when the beggar child extended an arm he gave it away on impulse. When Sujata looked their way the deed had been done.

Sukanta could see on her face the anger building up within. There would be an explosion if he spoke. Past experience held him back.

She was smouldering like a pile of cowdung cakes into which an ember had been dropped. What a man she had been married to! He was all right in other respects but the sight of someone suffering from hunger drove him mad. He was quite capable of giving away to

Translated from the Odia story 'Megha,' published in *Taraluthiba Samaya*, Bharata Bharati, Cuttack, 2010.

a beggar food that was still cooking on the hearth. It had happened more than once. But today's incident was not to be tolerated. What else was this but madness?

Two years ago, when they were living in Puri, *mahaprasad* had been brought from the temple. Her mother had come from the village on a visit. Sukanta, the children and she had eaten but her mother did not eat because of a stomach upset. Sujata carefully saved some mahaprasad for her mother.

FIGURE 3. 'WAIT, MY CHILD. I WILL COOK THIS RICE FOR YOU AT ONCE.'

It was a Sunday, nearly two in the afternoon. Sukanta came to her and said, 'Sujata, is there anything to eat?'

'You know I didn't cook today because we were having mahaprasad,' she replied.

'No, no, I mean some snacks—some *chooda*, *moodhi* or biscuits. Anything.'

'No, there's nothing in the house,' she said. 'I'll go to the market in the evening and get something. But why do you ask? It can't be because you need something to eat; you had lunch only an hour ago.'

'No, there's an old woman outside asking for food,' he said. 'Poor thing, she looks really hungry.'

'Well, tell her to go elsewhere. We are not running a free kitchen,' she said.

He said nothing but moved away from the bedroom slowly.

It was 3 o'clock when she got up to get some mahaprasad for her mother. There was none. She was wild with anger. She lost control and right there, in the verandah, in the presence of her mother and the children, she gave him a piece of her mind. Everyone was shocked.

Sukanta said not a word. But that night he said he wasn't feeling well and did not eat. He lay on his side all night.

Next morning she found his pillow damp. He had been crying.

On her mother's advice, she begged him to forgive her. Things slowly returned to normal.

She couldn't understand his utter lack of worldly wisdom. Did he have to strip himself naked in order to prove his generosity? Then why had he got married and taken on the responsibilities of a family?

The Bhubaneswar–Raipur Intercity had been launched only recently and didn't have a pantry car. Moreover, it halted very briefly at stations, not allowing enough time for one to run and buy food from a kiosk.

Sujata's stomach was churning with hunger. She felt faint. How could he be so thoughtless?

Neither of them spoke. The train entered Bhubaneswar station at 9.30. They got off and went straight to their home in Shastri Nagar. Sukanta had a bath and went off to the bank where he worked. He hadn't taken even a drop of water.

Sujata was still in a sulk. Her anger would not subside. Enough is enough, she was thinking; I can't take it any more. The children have grown up: our daughter is married and living in Bangalore and our son works in Hyderabad. Let them get a little more settled in life and then he can be as charitable as he wants.

She drank a glass of water and stretched out on the bed. No cooking for her and no lunch.

And Sukanta? He took half the day off and came home early. On the way he stopped at a South Indian restaurant and had meals packed for the two of them. He knew Sujata wouldn't have had anything to eat.

Yes, he had been rather thoughtless. He had got the biscuits specially for Sujata; he should have saved at least a couple when he gave the packet away. He blamed himself.

The door was open when he reached home. In her anger, she had forgotten to close it. He walked into the bedroom and said, 'Suji, I'm hungry. There are two meals for us on the dining table. Come, let's eat. I'm really sorry for what happened.'

She was weak with hunger and didn't speak. She got up, unpacked the parcel of food, served it in two trays and started eating without waiting for him.

Lunch was eaten without a word being said. Sujata had a glass of water and returned to the bed. It was 2.30 in the afternoon. The morning had been hot but there were clouds in the sky now. A cold breeze was blowing. The rain would come down any minute.

Though she wasn't feeling sleepy she closed her eyes and lay on the bed in a sullen mood.

She knew he had no faults as a husband. He wasn't short-tempered; he wasn't careless with money. He had never looked at another woman. He didn't know what liquor was. He was fiercely attached to the children and was like a son to her parents. Her mother-in-law was already old when she married Sukanta. She had lost her husband ages ago and guarded her son like a treasure. Her only daughter had died early. It was a poor family that Sukanta had come from, but he had been meritorious. Now he was the manager in a bank. All very well—but how were they to manage if he never looked after his own interests? If he insisted on giving away the food on his own plate? Their daughter said, 'Mother, Father is god-like. You should try to understand him.' She would retort angrily, 'What is there to understand? He shouldn't have had children if he wanted to become a god. At my cost!'

She saw Sukanta lying flat on his bed, gripping the pillow in his hand.

This is something new; I've never seen him sleeping in the daytime. All he can ever think of is his work, even on a Sunday. How strange to see him in bed at this time! She was beginning to melt.

The sky had grown dark.

Suddenly, he said in a soft voice, 'Suji, have you gone to sleep? Listen, I'll tell you of an incident in our village.'

She did not reply but let him know through the slight movements of her body that she wasn't asleep.

He began, 'There was a poor family in the village, just like ours. They managed somehow on scraps and odds and ends. One son and one daughter; the son was older by two years. When the daughter was only a year old, the father died of cholera. What was the poor mother to do? They were high-caste Brahmins; she couldn't wash utensils in someone's home or work on someone's farm. The poor woman would go out while it was still dark and pound rice or make roast moodhi for someone. If a Brahmin neighbour's home had been "polluted" by a death or childbirth in the family, she would go and perform the ritual worship of the household deities and bring home the little rice that she received as payment. That was how she fed her two children.'

Sukanta became silent after he had said all this. His voice sounded hoarse. He gathered himself together and began again. Sujata was listening closely.

'Her son was three and a half years old and the daughter a year and a half. She was very sickly. Her brother took great care of her, protecting her like a shadow, because their mother had to go out and work. But the daughter wouldn't stop crying; the mother had a hard time calming her.

'There was a terrible famine that year. There was no government relief then as there is now. No matter how hard she worked, the mother could never find enough food for her children.

'One day, there was no food at all in the house. The girl cried for food from morning to night. The son was writhing in hunger too but how could he cry? Hadn't he been made responsible for his sister? He would get water from a pot frequently, drink it himself and make her drink.

'Their mother returned late at night with a handful of rice-husk tied into a knot in the end of her sari. She took the girl in her lap and caressed her. "Wait, my child," she said, "I'll cook this rice for you at once. Just be a little patient." "Mother, I'm hungry!" was all that the girl could say.

'The mother sat down in front of the hearth to cook the rice-husk she had brought. Her son sat quietly, watching the pot boil. The mother spread half of the sari she was wearing on the floor and laid the girl down. The child fell asleep, fatigued by her own crying.

'The rice was cooked. The mother didn't leave the place once. She poured out the rice into a bronze plate to let it cool. She looked at her son, looked at her daughter. The boy looked back at her with piteous eyes but the daughter had fallen asleep.

'"Wake up, my child, my treasure!" the mother called out. "Food is ready. Come and eat!"

'But the girl did not get up. The mother laid her hand on the child's shoulder to wake her up. The body was cold. She wasn't there any more.'

Sukanta suddenly broke down, unable to control himself. His body was shaken with sobs.

Sujata got up at once. She took her husband in her arms and held him tightly.

The rain poured down.

Any visitor to that home would have seen a grown man and woman in each other's arms, weeping together. The clouds were streaming down.

7. Freedom Fifty Saloon

There was a card lying on the table. An invitation card.

Chakradhar had come home and delivered it while I was out.

I was surprised on getting the invitation. Chakradhar was launching his own 'hairdressing saloon' in Bhubaneswar. 'Freedom Fifty Saloon' he had named it.

He was my childhood friend: we had been together from the Lower Primary to the matriculation class. Neither of us could be described as a good student but he always ranked eight or ten places below me. I believe that each one of us receives at birth an account book in which the story of one's life is inscribed in geometrical lines. Well, all I can say is that there were no straight lines in Chakradhar's book. He was clever and capable—I won't call him cunning since he was my friend. But he always said, 'Look, friend, there is cleverness in my blood, but it can't find expression yet. But you'll see how it blooms one day.'

Sometimes he would advise me, like an elder, 'You could do well in your studies if you applied yourself.'

Seeing our friendship, Sridhar Master, our teacher, would say, 'One day, the two of you are going to re-write the Abalokara story.* Chakradhar will be Abalokara and you'll be Gosain, his scribe, writing his story.'

There must have been some truth in what he said. At that time, I was writing songs for some of the cultural programmes in our school. Sridhar Master taught us Literature and I showed him a few of my creations, with Chakradhar accompanying me.

* The Abalokara stories are the Odia counterparts of the legendary Birbal–Akbar tales.

Translated from the Odia story 'Freedom Fifty Saloon,' published in *Taraluthiba Samaya*, Bharata Bharati, Cuttack, 2010.

Sridhar Master would offer a number of suggestions in response to my writing and it was Chakradhar who replied on my behalf. Sridhar Master was amused by what Chakradhar had to say and would comment, 'Chakra is a vagabond!'

And now *that* Chakradhar had invited me to the inauguration of his hairdressing saloon.

I read through the card again, carefully. The inauguration was on 30 January, Mahatma Gandhi's death anniversary. The Chief Minister himself would perform the inauguration and the Chief Guest on the occasion would be the well-known Gandhian and freedom fighter, Mohan Sharma. The most intriguing fact of all was that the saloon would provide services *gratis* to freedom fighters—in other words, give them free shaves and haircuts.

It was an expensive card. Exquisitely printed. The Chief Minister would do the honours. The saloon would be air-conditioned.

I felt stunned on reading the card. Where did the penniless Chakradhar acquire so much wealth in the meantime that he could start a sophisticated air-conditioned saloon? How did he get access to the Chief Minister? And what profits could he hope to make after he had given free shaves to all the freedom fighters in the state?

My mind refused to take all this in.

My eagerness to meet Chakradhar was increasing. Today was the 25th of January. Still five days to the event.

I am a lecturer in a college in Bhubaneswar, living in quarters provided by the government—Chakradhar had surely kept himself informed of all this, or else how could he have located my residence and delivered the invitation? Yet our last meeting had been eight years ago! I had hardly been to the village after my father's death, and so had not met Chakradhar for some time.

After I matriculated I moved to Cuttack and got admitted to a college while Chakradhar stayed on in the village. I met him very occasionally when I went there. He used to accompany his father, Sudei Barik (barber) from door to door. Sudei had clients in five neighbouring villages. Apart from attending to daily needs like haircuts and shaves, his services were in demand on a variety of occasions: weddings, sacred-thread ceremonies, ear-piercings, nose-piercings, funerals and obsequies, fasts and feasts. He was permanently on call in five villages and, not surprisingly, the owner of seven acres of land and a mango-orchard containing some twenty trees.

Life was smooth for Chakradhar's family but while I was in college his father was carried off in middle age by some disease. They had to sell some of their land and suddenly their troubles intensified. Being the eldest son in a multi-branched family Chakradhar was forced to shoulder the family's burdens. He had to take up razor and brush.

But that he would come to Bhubaneswar and start a modern hairdressing saloon was beyond my reckoning.

He lived in the village, got married and set up his own family. We met whenever I went to the village and he would inquire after me but not once did he tell me how he was managing and I felt no need to ask. What startling change could be expected in the life of a village barber? But he was obviously good at his job.

He was active in village politics as well. He had built up excellent social relationships and had kept himself well informed about all that was happening in the world. Sometimes he would begin a discussion in his own way, using newspaper headlines as his base. But I did not like his garrulousness at all; it seemed unwarranted.

If you inhabit the earth you should be talking of the trees around you, the wind and rain; if you talk of clouds, sky and stars instead, who would like to listen? That's the kind of person Chakradhar was. He would forget the fish in the pond nearby and start plucking flowers in the sky.

I remembered his childhood boast: 'There's cleverness in my blood!' The country became independent in 1947; we would soon be completing fifty years of freedom. Various national programmes had been started to celebrate the Silver Jubilee of Independence; the country's economy, its social, political and material progress were being hotly debated; poets and writers were composing books—and here Chakradhar had found a new form of celebration! The 'Freedom Fifty Saloon.' The culmination of fifty years of Independence!

My curiosity was aroused.

One had to admire what he was doing. A rustic he might have been, but who could question his inventiveness!

There may be hundreds of hairdressing saloons in Bhubaneswar. Are the margins of profit so high that he could afford to take such a risk? Bank loans are easy to get now—true; but what new tricks of the trade had Chakradhar, our village barber, learnt that people would crowd into his saloon? And to crown everything—free shaves and haircuts for freedom fighters!

His scheme was bound to fail. The inevitable end of all those who are too clever for their own good.

This trait of his had earned him a thrashing once from our Headmaster. When he was in the ninth class, he thought up a new scheme on a sudden inspiration—a lottery. He called it the 'Poor Man's Door to Wealth.' He told everyone that the lottery would be made available to the entire school. Each student could buy a lottery ticket for fifty paise and the youngest child in the school would draw lots in the presence of everyone. The person whose name came up would get the prize of a hundred rupees.

By Chakradhar's calculation, at least two hundred and fifty of the three hundred and fifty students in the school would buy tickets, and at fifty paise a ticket, that would amount to a hundred and twenty-five rupees, leaving a margin of twenty-five rupees for him. Not bad at all!

But the Headmaster was furious. 'No gambling in my school!' he roared. 'Where is that Chakradhar? Bring him here!' That was the end of Chakradhar's masterly scheme.

Was the Freedom Fifty Saloon story going to be similar?

I waited for the 30th of January.

I had not thought it necessary to investigate, in the meantime, what Chakradhar had been up to.

On that day, I reached the Convent School Crossing on Janpath at exactly the right time. The 'saloon' stood by the road-side, at a little distance. The large signboard, in Odia, declared 'Freedom Fifty Saloon.' The name might be in a foreign language but the script was patriotic. One had to give Chakradhar full marks!

Huge floral garlands all around. A broad red ribbon tied across the doorway. A *shamiana* in front. Soft music over the PA. Rows of red plastic chairs, from some agency.

The auspicious time for the inauguration was precisely thirty minutes past ten. It is now fifteen past. The Chief Minister will arrive any minute. The Chief Guest has already arrived. Policemen on patrol, blowing their whistles.

The Odisha Legislative Assembly is in winter session. But the Chief Minister has given his word; he will come but for only fifteen minutes.

Chakradhar suddenly appeared out of nowhere and came rushing to my side. Held me tight, his voice choking. Dragged me into the crowd. Introduced me to Mohan Sharma, Chief Guest, many others as well, declaring I was a well-known professor. Most people in spotless *khadi*. Chakradhar wore a loose *punjabi* over tight blue jeans, with black *chappals* on his feet.

This new Chakradhar bore little resemblance to the friend I had known: his appearance, his speech, his very face seemed unfamiliar. But my right hand was gripped in his warm palm.

The Chief Minister arrived just then. Chakradhar ran to touch his feet. Smiling faintly, the Chief Minister patted him on the back, then walked on with his hand on Chakradhar's shoulder.

The ribbon was cut. Applause.

In a brief speech, the Chief Minister said, 'The future of democracy in this country is bright. It is our Chakradhars who will carry the country forward. The determination to stand on one's own feet and reverence for those who have made the supreme sacrifice for the country will surely carry us into a new dawn.'

The Chief Guest, Mohan Sharma, renowned freedom fighter, broke into tears while felicitating Chakradhar. 'Such devotion to freedom fighters is rare among the youth of the new generation,' he declared. 'Chakradhar*ji* is an ideal for today's youth.'

More applause. I joined in. Chakradhar was like a flower in full bloom.

Sweets were distributed.

Slowly, the meeting drew to a close. I was planning to slip away unseen.

Just then Chakradhar gripped me by the hand. 'Why don't you sit down for a while?' he said. 'I know you have to go, but what's the hurry? You are my only friend here; most of the others I don't even know.'

His affection was infectious. I felt encouraged to ask the question that lurked in my heart. 'Tell me, Chakradhar, what is all this? You have started a saloon at such great expense, and on top of that you have announced free services for freedom fighters! Are you bent on self-destruction?'

He laughed. 'What a simpleton you are!' he said. 'Why should I suffer? The bank has given me a loan. That old man, Mohan Sharma, is the guarantor. This land and building belong to another freedom fighter. There is no one to inherit his property. As for the freedom fighters whom I have promised my services free, have you counted how many there are? Most of them are dry leaves waiting to fall—they will have no need to visit my saloon. Some are bald and the others have beards. And if someone does turn up, he will be my publicity agent! I will give him such an oil-massage that he will go around declaring, "There is no one in the world like Chakradhar Barik!" You know, there is a powerful OBC storm sweeping through the country now. In a few years, seats will be reserved in the State Assembly for OBC candidates, along with the SCs and STs. And is there anyone in our region, apart from me, who is qualified?'

Having made his speech in a single breath, he looked at me.

His eyes were shining. I recalled his childhood boast: 'Just wait for this flower to bloom!'

And as Sridhar Master had predicted, I was waiting to write the new Abalokara story.

Note: The word in use now is 'salon.' In South Asia, a barber's shop is still known as a 'saloon.' The Oxford Dictionary mentioned 'hairdressing saloon' even in the 1980s.

OBC, or, Other Backward Class, is a collective term used by the Government of India to classify people who are educationally and socially disadvantaged, apart from the Scheduled Castes (SCs) and Scheduled Tribes (STs).

8. God's Creation

Pranab spent much of his time pursuing all kinds of strange and quite unnecessary ideas, to Basanti's great exasperation. 'Why do you have to get involved in things that don't concern you?' she would tell him. 'What is it to you whether someone's son or daughter gets a job or not?' But he ignored her protestations. 'Sudam Babu's son should have studied Engineering rather than Medicine,' he would declare. Or 'Manmohan Singh made a mistake by agreeing to become Prime Minister'; 'Odisha's borders should have been drawn differently'; 'It should have rained today instead of yesterday.' Such were the complex issues that kept his mind engaged. Sometimes he would become so agitated that he would itch to find someone to share his concerns with. But who was there in the house apart from Basanti? The poor lady would get drawn into every problem—and then the debate and shouting would begin. 'Whatever God does is always for the best,' she would insist. 'All that has happened is right and whatever is going to happen will be equally just. You keep out of it! It's time for the office now—go and get ready. Mind your own business and don't try to play God!'

But he wouldn't give up. Let Basanti shout! It wasn't as if his meddlesome nature didn't cause problems at the office. Some, however, praised him. One day the boss's secretary said with a smile,'Pranab Babu, you are a thinking person!' He smiled back at her—it was how he liked to think of himself.

Only the other day, the thought suddenly came to him that the *kankad*, one of his favourite vegetables, should have been smooth on the outside rather than furry. He tried to explain to his colleagues the advantages that could have accrued from this

Translated from the Odia story 'Eeswaranka Samsara,' published in *Taraluthiba Samaya*, Bharata Bharati, Cuttack, 2010.

improved configuration of the fruit. They listened in silence, without comment—but lack of audience participation never held Pranab back.

This happened quite long ago—maybe ten or twelve years back. Pranab had been posted to Baripada then. He lived in a small rented house on Baghda Road. His neighbour was Ghanshyam Patel, or Ghana Babu, a clerk in the Civil Supplies Department. Pranab's two sons were in high school, as were Ghana Babu's daughter and son. The two families were close to each other. On returning from the bank, Pranab would call across the fence, 'Come, Ghana Babu, let's have tea together,' and Ghana Babu never refused.

FIGURE 4. THERE'S A BRIDE FOR EVERY GROOM AND FOR EVERY BRIDE THERE'S A GROOM.

They would chat for hours over tea, with Ghana Babu providing the chorus to Pranab's spirited performances. 'You are quite right! That's how it should have been!' he would say, or, 'Who can be sure that the situation won't change?' encouraging him to rise to new heights of eloquence. There could not have been a more accomplished listener and so Pranab and he made an ideal pair.

One day it suddenly occurred to Pranab that Kuma would never be able to get married. Kuma was Ghana Babu's only daughter. He brought up the matter himself as he was going to bed. Surprisingly, Basanti did not react strongly, as she usually did. 'That's true,' she said quietly. 'Poor girl!'

Kuma was the top student in her class and was blessed with a sweet and gentle nature. Everyone who came to know her well was charmed and both Pranab and Basanti were extremely fond of her. Nevertheless, it would be difficult for her to find a match in a society where every son was looked upon as an asset and every daughter a liability—especially if Nature had been less than kind. No one grumbled if a prospective son-in-law was dark or overweight, but a future daughter-in-law could expect to be scrutinised under a microscope. The slightest imperfection—and she was doomed to be a burden to her parents all her life.

Basanti said, 'You know, I feel so sad when I think of Ghana Babu and Sula Nani, his wife—they're such wonderful people, so anxious to help others. With just one son and a daughter they should have had no worries, but with poor Kuma in the house ... How unjust God is sometimes! Why is such a good soul as Sula Nani being punished in this way?'

Pranab and Basanti often discussed Kuma's marriage and they agreed that her prospects were not bright at all. But Ghanshyam Babu and Sula Nani were never told of these confabulations. 'It's such a sensitive matter!' Pranab would say, and Basanti chipped in with, 'Who doesn't have problems? But unpleasant truths must never be told!'

Pranab and Ghanshyam Babu were neighbours in Baripada for almost five years. Ideal neighbours, living side by side in absolute harmony. Then suddenly one day, Pranab received orders of transfer. He had been promoted, but he was being posted outside the state, to Nagpur. A year later, Ghanshyam Babu was transferred to Nabarangpur. The link between the two families was broken. No one wrote letters now: it was the age of mobile telephones.

But telephone numbers changed so quickly that it was impossible to keep track. As a result, Pranab and Ghanshyam Babu never communicated with each other, but each family was remembered often by the other with affection. Once in a while Basanti would say to Pranab, 'We never tried to find out if Kuma got married, did we? It has been a long time ...'

'I'm afraid she may be unmarried still,' Pranab said. 'If her complexion had been a few shades lighter ...' And Basanti would shout, 'There you go again! Is there anything you could have done?'

With the passage of time the topic of Kuma's marriage lost much of its interest. Pranab's own world had expanded; his two sons were working now and the elder one was married. He lived in Bangalore with his wife. Pranab himself was back in Bhubaneswar.

One day, Pranab and Basanti happened to be in Puri. After they had offered their prayers in the Jagannath temple Basanti proposed, 'Let's go and have a look at the beach. I hear the sea has washed away part of it.' Pranab had no choice but to follow.

There weren't too many people at the beach. The sea was calm but occasionally the breeze would fling a handful of sand into your face. Pranab and Basant sat down on the sand. Suddenly Pranab said, 'You know, Basanti, if Puri town had been facing north and south instead of east and west ...' Before he could finish, Basanti suddenly shouted out, 'Look, look! Isn't that our Ghanshyam Babu?'

Pranab saw, at a distance, Ghanshyam Babu trudging along the seashore, followed by Sula Nani. 'Not just Ghanshyam Babu,' he said, excited, 'There's your Sula Nani too!'

'Let's go and meet them!' said Basanti, and simultaneously she stood up and started running. The two couples met enthusiastically. Embraced; inquired about each other's welfare. Ghanshyam Babu was living in Bhubaneswar as well, and he too was on a visit to Puri.

Suddenly Basanti said to Sula Nani, 'Nani, what news of Kuma?'

'Kuma? There she is!' Sula Nani said, pointing. 'That's her husband behind her. They have been married four years now. We couldn't send you an invitation as we didn't know where you were.'

Basanti saw Kuma walking towards them across the beach. She had put on weight since they had last seen her. Behind her was her husband. They made a matched pair and were obviously happy.

Later that night, Pranab said to Basanti, 'God looks after everyone, doesn't He? There's a bride for every groom and for every bride there's a groom. That's the beauty of God's creation. Now, if only Kuma's marriage had taken place while we were in Baripada ...'

'Keep quiet, will you?' Basanti said. 'You are not God, you know!'

9. Gold

It was 12.30 in the afternoon—time for classes to end. Parents were waiting outside the school to meet their children and take them home. The bell rang and the children rushed out. But they were in no hurry to go home. This was the time they enjoyed most, playing with their friends.

I was waiting for Jinu, my four-year old daughter. I tried to locate her in that crowd of children but they all looked alike in their blue uniforms. Then I saw her. She was busy talking to another child—in fact, to *three* other children, of roughly the same age as herself. Jinu can never stop talking; she must be the most talkative child in the world. When I was a child I tried to think of ways to avoid going to school, but Jinu would get terribly upset if someone told her, 'Your school is closed today' or 'It's raining, you can't go to school.'

Like other parents, my wife and I were anxious that our children should do well at school. My son, who was nine, had been made to join two coaching classes and my wife spent two hours with Jinu every evening, making sure she got her spellings right. We felt it was never too early for any child to understand the seriousness of studies.

But Jinu was a rebel. Friends meant everything to her; that was what school was all about. She did not even look at me now. But her friend Runi, who is the daughter of a neighbour, came to me with her eyes full of tears. 'Uncle, uncle,' she cried, 'Jinu pushed me today. Look!' and she showed me a small cut on one knee.

Jinu saw me at last and ran to me. I asked her, trying to sound gentle, 'Jinu, did you push Runi? You shouldn't have done that!'

Translated from the Odia story 'Suna,' published in *Akshyara Aranya*, Bharata Bharati, Cuttack, 1994.

'No, Daddy, I didn't push her,' she said breathlessly. 'She tried to snatch it from my hand and I told her I won't give it to her but she didn't listen and snatched it away and I ...'

Runi was crying uncontrollably. I thought Jinu had taken away something that belonged to her. 'Jinu,' I said, 'if Runi wants something, why don't you give it to her? You shouldn't quarrel with your friend.'

Now it was Jinu's turn to burst into tears. 'No, Daddy, I won't, I won't!' she howled.

I decided not to pursue the matter. 'Come, Jinu,' I said, leading her towards my scooter, 'we will go home!' I signalled to Runi not to worry, that everything would be all right.

When we reached home and Jinu had put away her bag and changed her clothes I asked her, 'Jinu darling, what was it that Runi wanted? Did you take something that belongs to her?'

'No, Daddy,' she shouted, 'it's mine, not hers! I found it! It was lying in the grass and I saw it first but she said she wanted it, but why should I give it to her?'

'Very well, Jinu, don't give it to her if you don't want to,' I said. 'But what is it?'

'A piece of gold!' Juni said. 'I'm going to keep it in my wooden box. It's mine!'

Gold? A four-year old girl? How could she know what gold is?

I had to find out what it was. That afternoon, when Jinu was sleeping, I went to the room where she kept her things. There was a little desk there, which Jinu called her 'wooden box.' Here she had hidden away all her treasures—silver-coloured chocolate wrappers, bits of worn-out crayons, coloured pebbles ... and what was obviously her most recent acquisition. A tiny piece of glass. Golden in colour. Her gold.

I felt so relieved—like someone who has walked, unknowingly, into a garden full of flowers, after trudging all day through crowded city streets.

10. Gurudakshina

Nilambar Babu's grandson came and said: 'There's a money order for you, Jejey. Postman *Mousa* is calling you.'

Nilambar Babu was reading *Mathura Mangala*. He placed his glasses on top of the open book, got up and came to the front door. Who could have sent me a money order, he thought, perplexed.

He had retired ten years ago. Neither of his two sons lived with him. He had acquired a small grocery shop in the village and found a teacher's job in the local school. His married daughter lived nearby. Then who could have sent him money? Not a paltry hundred or a thousand—a full five thousand.

'Postman Babu,' he said, moderately excited, 'it could be for someone else. Will you check the address again?' But the postman was quite certain—the money was for Nilambar Babu.

'Who is it from?' Nilambar Babu asked again.

Some Basanta Kumar Lenka, whose address was given as Assistant Teacher, Mirzapur High School, Mirzapur, Bonai. With wrinkled forehead, dancing eyebrows and speculative fingers combing through his thin hair, Nilambar Babu searched through jumbled memories, past and present, but of Basanta Kumar Lenka he found no trace. There is a tiny space at the bottom of every money order form and there Nilambar Babu saw the scribble, 'A small *gurudakshina* from me. Yours, Basanta.' How strange! Who was this Basanta and why had he sent all this money? What was his objective?

It seemed unreal. He hesitated to accept the money from the postman but was obliged to, finally. Still he didn't feel it belonged to him.

Translated from the Odia story 'Gurudakshina,' published in *Sparsha* (Magazine—Puja Special), 2012.

What was he to do with the money? Spend it or wait, in case some other person's money order had come to him by mistake? In that case, it would be awkward for him if the money had been spent. Confused, he put it away in a box. He didn't mention it to anyone. Who knew—there might be complications.

The five thousand rupees remained in the box.

The incident had an unsettling impact on Nilambar Babu's placid life. He began living in a state of anxiety. Somebody might turn up someday and demand, 'That money order was for me!' Or someone might remove the money from the box without his knowledge. Who could be trusted? He couldn't talk to anyone about it. His wife had died three years ago. If the money had really been his, he would have handed it over to her. But that could never be.

What a troubled childhood he had had! What poverty he had faced! Two years in his own village, then four years in his maternal uncle's village, followed by another four as a cook in somebody's house in Puri, so that he could work his way through school; then the year in the Elementary Teacher Training School in Raipur, before he was appointed teacher in a primary school. And next, marriage and family life.

He had served in seven schools before returning to his village to retire as a Headmaster. A lifetime spent in study and teaching. That, and the love of students, were all he had ever known. Every student was like his own child.

People who were familiar with his style of teaching wondered why he didn't write books for children. He had never tried; but now he often thought, if he *had* written books, he could have got some money in his old age. A meagre pension was all the income he had. There was hardly any land to speak of.

But who could have sent that money? Who had thought of sending him a gurudakshina ten years after his retirement?

Then Nilambar Babu remembered something. While he had been a teacher in Raipur Middle English School, a jeep had stopped in front of his house one day. Somebody stepped out of the jeep, climbed up the steps that led to his verandah, bowed low and touched his feet in a gesture of reverence. It was an old student of his who had become a senior engineer. He had brought a large packet of sweets. But his name had been Mukunda Mahapatra. Who was Basanta Kumar Lenka then? He couldn't remember anything about him. No letter had ever come from him.

Then one day, when Nilambar Babu was sitting quietly in his verandah, gazing vacantly at the sky, the postman brought him a letter. It was from the same Basanta Kumar Lenka. He tore open the envelope and began to read the letter.

It said:

> Respected Nilambar *Saar*,
>
> Kindly accept my humble *pranam*. I hope and trust you are well. I was a student of Class 7 when you were a teacher in Khurda Middle English School, twenty-five years ago. I have been trying for several years to get your address and have just learnt from a colleague that you are living in your village after retirement. After a great deal of thought, I sent you a money order. I was not sure if it would reach you, but felt relieved on seeing your signature on the receipt. With that, a heavy burden that I have been carrying for twenty-five years has been lifted. I was wondering where you were, how you were, how I could meet you and clutch your feet and beg forgiveness. Today, I am writing to express my joy. You have brought peace to my mind by accepting that money. I have decided to meet you in person next summer. For the present, I am living, with my wife and children, in distant Bonaigarh, where I am posted.

It was a long letter, written in a neat hand. He tried to recall the years in Khurda. But he had no memory at all of a student named Basanta. What was the burden on Basanta's head? What had been his own role in it?

Then he had a doubt again. Had the letter been addressed to the right Nilambar? Or was there another?

He read on.

Basanta had written,

> Saar, I beg you not to misunderstand me. If you cannot think of the money as a gurudakshina offered at your feet, please think of it as a *pranami* and accept it for your personal use. I am quite sure you would not have touched the money so far. But if you do not accept it and use it for yourself, I shall be pained.

To Nilambar Babu, it was still a mystery. What a peculiar creature he was—this Basanta Kumar Lenka. Just because Nilambar Babu had taught him something in some forgotten past, he had sent him a gurudakshina and was compelling him to spend the money on himself. How strange.

He turned the page.

Saar, perhaps you remember that you always had a bag in your hand while walking to the school. Whenever you saw fresh vegetables or greens being sold by the wayside, you bought some and put them in your bag. You carried them to the school. Sometimes, when you saw a student, you would say, 'Son, will you take these vegetables to my home and give them to my wife?' Since you were everyone's favourite teacher, why would anyone refuse? The boys went willingly, in that hot sun, to your house two kilometres away.

I had a friend named Sudama. We were the two most mischievous boys in the class and were regularly scolded by all the teachers. You never said anything to us but sometimes, when you had bought something, you would ask us to deliver it at your home. You always asked us to bring the bag back. We were compelled to sit in the classroom after we had returned the bag to you, or else we would have gone roaming like the vagabonds we were.

Once, when you were returning from the market with a bagful of vegetables, you saw us and said, 'Boys, will you take this bag to my home? There's still some time before class begins.'

It was the height of summer. We did not like what you said. Sudama said to me, 'The old man treats us like coolies. Let's teach him a lesson.' I agreed. We always thought you wanted to humiliate us because we weren't good students. So we decided to hire a rickshaw to take us to your home and back and get our *guru ma* to pay the fare. I remember, when we delivered the bag to her and said, 'The rickshaw-puller has to be paid five rupees and Saar has asked you to pay the fare,' she looked surprised but said nothing and gave us a five-rupee note. We returned to school proudly riding that rickshaw, thinking we had won a great victory. We thought, 'After his wife has told him what happened, the old man will never ask us to carry his bag again.' And in fact, you never did.

But it pained us that you did not scold us for what we had done, though you must have been told of it. Several times, I wanted to go to you and beg forgiveness, but it never happened. The next year you were transferred out of Khurda. But the guilt has remained in my mind, weighing me down.

I don't know why, but after I had become a teacher, years later, I constantly thought of you. One day an old classmate from the Khurda days told me, 'I met Nilambar Saar recently. He looks just the same as before.'

I couldn't say anything. But I tell you honestly, Saar, it was as if the poison of humiliation spread through my veins. I felt ashamed of myself. Following your ideals, I have never spoken harshly to any student. It was your smiling face that I remembered always.

I have planned often to search you out, but other matters always prevented me. It is only now that I realise, when I have become a teacher, how much you loved your students. Your loving way of teaching is such a beautiful memory.

I tell myself always—I cheated not only my Saar but also my guru ma and took five rupees from her by deceit. I have always repented my act and feel I must make amends. But if I say that sending the money order was my act of penance, I know you will never accept it. The five thousand rupees, therefore, is my gurudakshina. I beg you to accept it so that my mind may find peace.

Your obedient pupil,

Basanta.

Nilambar Babu's eyes grew moist after he had read the letter. The faces of many old pupils floated up through the tears. He went into the house and sat down on the cot with eyes closed and remained seated for a long time.

The next day, a money order was sent to Basanta Kumar Lenka, Assistant Teacher, Mirzapur High School, Bonai. It was for four thousand nine hundred and ninety-five rupees. In the space at the bottom, Nilambar Babu had written:

Dear Basanta, my best wishes to you. What a student takes from his teacher is his by right. No interest is payable. So, five rupees cannot grow into five thousand. For your peace of mind, however, I have retained five rupees. The fact that you have been repenting for the small mistake you made that day is sufficient gurudakshina. You must come and see me during the next summer vacation. My blessings to your children.

Yours,

Nilambar Satpathi

11. The Harmonium

Sudhakar couldn't believe his own eyes. Chuni was singing and that too on TV! How beautifully she was singing! Why had no one told him she had turned into an accomplished singer? Surely, Purnima must have known! But she hadn't breathed a word to him.

He felt hurt. After a few minutes of silence he called out to Purnima. She was busy in the kitchen. As she walked towards him, wiping her hands, Sudhakar said, 'Come and see—isn't that our Chuni? Why did no one tell me she sang on TV?'

Purnima said gravely, 'Yes, it's Chuni! I knew she was taking music lessons from a famous *ustad* in Delhi. "Don't tell Father," she begged me, "he won't approve! But what could I do—Sukanta insisted! We'd gone on a picnic one day with some friends and their families and everyone had to sing! I was forced to sing too and after I had sung someone said, 'Why, Sukanta, you have a Lata Mangeshkar hidden away at home! Why weren't we told earlier?' I felt so embarrassed! The moment we returned home, Sukanta announced, 'Your music lessons start tomorrow!' I wasn't given a choice!"'

'Yes, but she could have told me she was a TV artiste!'

'How could she? Do you realise what a terror you've been to the children all your life? Have you ever allowed them any freedom at all? Discipline, the family's reputation—that's all you've cared about! It's a miracle my children didn't have their spirits broken!'

She began to sob, overcome by emotions which she had kept locked up for years. Sudhakar said nothing; there was no denying his guilt. In another year he would retire from the bank. Now there was only Purnima to keep him company; the children had married

Translated from the Odia story 'Harmonium,' published in *Taraluthiba Samaya*, Bharata Bharati, Cuttack, 2010.

and moved away. They were all comfortably off. Was it only their own efforts that had seen them through? It was hard to tell. But Purnima's accusation hurt.

Sudhakar was afloat on his own current, groping to find himself in his own darkness.

He had faced a great deal of stress in life, connected mostly with his family. He was easily upset. His home was his pot of milk; the slightest rise in temperature could bring it to a boil.

FIGURE 5. 'IS THIS WHAT YOU TEACH A GIRL STUDYING IN THE FIFTH CLASS?'

Had he been to blame? Losing one's calm easily was a family trait. His grandmother had said it of his grandfather and his mother had kept repeating it about her husband. And now Purnima had started the same chant.

But wasn't it his fault that the children never communicated with him? Discipline was necessary, true—but one had to learn how to be flexible. A mother was like the earth—the mould in which the body was shaped, while the father was the sky, providing a protective shield, but at a distance; giving out a warning flash of lightning or growl of thunder when necessary. But it had to be a gentle rumble, not a steady roar. Maybe he had never realised this. In his arrogance and anger, he had been like a scorpion, injecting his own venom into himself. *It's all my fault*, he thought.

With moist eyes, he switched off the TV and lay down on the bed. Maybe tears would provide relief.

It had happened years ago—more than twenty, surely. Chuni was in the fifth grade then. The music lessons at home went on alongside her schooling. They had started two years ago at Purnima's insistence. She claimed a child must be initiated at the age of six. Sudhakar had not been enthusiastic but he had not resisted either. Very well, let it go on—as long as it didn't interfere with her studies. The music teacher came three days a week, for an hour in the evening. 'Look, Ma,' he would tell his pupil, 'you must rise early in the morning and practise what you were taught the night before. Saraswati has blessed you with a divine voice; all you need is practice.'

Even at that young age, Chuni understood her responsibilities. She would get up early and sit down on the bed to rehearse her music lessons, until Sudhakar came in and said, 'That's enough! Time for studies now!'

Purnima grumbled if these words fell into her ears. 'Study, study, study—that's all one hears! As if study was one's life breath!' That was all; Sudhakar would have proved difficult to manage if she had said more. It wasn't as though he didn't like music: the cassette-player and pile of cassettes on his desk proved that was not the case—but what mattered was discipline. If the children didn't do well in their studies, what future would they have?

After Chuni's music lessons had gone on for some months, her teacher said she should get a harmonium, and Purnima promptly obtained her husband's approval. When he went to Kolkata on work he brought home a beautiful harmonium from the famous Bani Company, made of mahogany. How it glistened! For a couple of days Chuni was delirious with joy.

The music teacher's visits became longer. He gave Chuni long lectures on raga and tala in addition to teaching her new songs. Sometimes Sudhakar overheard him. Once he heard the teacher say, 'Do you know, Ma, all the songs in the world are made up of just seven notes—*sa*, *re*, *ga*, *ma*, *pa*, *dha*, *ni*. We can find these notes all around us—they are there in the cries of animals and the songs of birds. "Sa" comes from "*shadaj*," the peacock; "re" comes from "*rishabh*," the bull, and so on.' Sudhakar listened with interest. He had never known there was so much wisdom behind music.

The music teacher was knowledgeable. Thin, dark and short-statured, with bobbed hair and a mouth that was constantly filled with paan. Probably used perfumed hair-oil; you could smell him at a distance. He wore a thin *punjabi* and *nagra* shoes on his feet. His eyes were lined with kohl, which gave him a theatrical look. A big blob of *sindoor* on his forehead—clearly a *rasik*, a man of taste.

The music teacher was properly looked after whenever he came—no slackness was allowed there. It was Purnima who managed everything; Sudhakar had no time for such things. But he never failed to caution the mother and the daughter, 'Look, nothing should affect her studies!'

The days went by; Chuni's music lessons continued and so did her classes at school. She had been learning music for three years now and could sing really well. That evening, it had been rather sultry after the rain. Purnima was seated in a chair in the verandah while Chuni's music lesson was in progress on the other side. The teacher was teaching her the words and tune of a new song. He would cue her with the opening words of each line and play the melody on the harmonium, and she would sing the line in tune.

Just then, Sudhakar walked in. Chuni was singing:

On the night of the new moon
The love of my life lay in my lap on the bed ...

He stormed into the room, his face flaming with anger. What was happening? Purnima stood up, frightened. Sudhakar pulled the harmonium out of the music teacher's hand, picked it up and threw it down on the floor. It gave out a dying whine and shattered. The music teacher was on his feet; his eyes were brimming but he said nothing.

'Is this what you teach a girl studying in the fifth class?' Sudhakar roared. 'You are a mature person—don't you have a little sense? Teaching the child all kinds of vulgarities in the name of music!'

He was fuming while Chuni trembled. The teacher stood with his face averted. Purnima was confused. What was she supposed to do?

'No more music lessons for Chuni!' was Sudhakar's closing salvo. To the teacher he said, 'You needn't come here again; I'll send you whatever money is due to you. Now go!' he shouted.

Neither Chuni nor Purnima knew when the teacher left. Purnima's sobbing filled the room. Ending the lessons was one thing—but did it have to be done so crudely? No one in her parents' home would have dreamt of such a thing. But Sudhakar was Sudhakar.

No words were spoken after the teacher left. The broken harmonium lay unnoticed. Chuni went to bed without eating a morsel.

After that day, Chuni's music lessons were a closed chapter. But when Sudhakar saw her sing on television, a medley of emotions rose within him. He was suddenly filled with loathing for himself. He could not look Purnima in the face. A shroud of defeat and dejection enveloped him.

Chuni had sung a Hindi song on television. She was good enough to sing on a national channel. His heart puffed up with pride. How his relations and friends would compliment him when they heard her! How well he had brought up his children, they would say.

But did he deserve any credit? He couldn't even praise Chuni in Purnima's presence. He felt himself sliding into some forgotten past.

But Purnima wasn't prepared to let the past go. She didn't say a word. If she had, Sudhakar would have admitted his fault and begged forgiveness. But she wasn't going to give him an opportunity.

Maybe that's the effect that ageing has on one. The seeds of the past blossomed into thorny cactuses. You couldn't grip them.

It was morning. Sudhakar said to Purnima, 'I think I'll go to Delhi next week for a few days. I would like to see Chuni.' Purnima showed no pleasure at his words. All she said was, 'Yes, you should go and see her.' She didn't ask why he wasn't asking her to accompany him.

Sudhakar arrived in Delhi. Chuni lived in an apartment in Vasant Kunj. He hadn't informed her he was coming. She opened the door and cried out excitedly 'Bapa!' He could see her only dimly through his tears.

She dragged his suitcase into the apartment. Then she asked, 'What's in that big box, Bapa?'

Flustered, he said, 'Don't refuse it, my child. I've got you a harmonium!' His tears were flowing.

Who could have controlled Chuni's tears then?

12. Kaanduri*

After Kaanduri was born, Bou never had a life of her own. On becoming a mother, every Indian woman is expected to dedicate her life completely to her children; nevertheless, she still has *some* freedom. But Kaanduri's arrival robbed my mother of any freedom that she might have had.

Her mornings invariably began at 4.00—rain or shine, summer or winter. This unwavering habit irritated me: what satisfaction did she get by sacrificing those blissful moments of pre-dawn sleep? But she seemed to be under a vow! Was it Kaanduri who had forced her to acquire the habit? Or had she willed it on herself?

As soon as she got out of bed, Bou would start working with feverish energy, running through the daily routine one step at a time: sprinkling cow-dung water around the courtyard, boiling paddy-husk to use as fodder for the cattle, scrubbing utensils, giving the floor of the puja room a fresh coat of mud plastering... When did she find time for her personal needs? But in the middle of all the household chores, one ear was constantly trained on Kaanduri lest she should wake up and start crying. The mother's instinct prevailed over the housewife's obligations. When I woke up in the morning, the Bou I saw was the same alert, energetic Bou I had seen the night before. Never any change—day after day, year after year.

When she had finished, she would pick Kaanduri up from the bed. On some days Kaanduri would start howling before Bou had had her bath. She could create an incredible hue and cry over the

* 'Kaanduri' is an Odia word, suggestive of derision as well as affection, used to describe a girl or woman who is always crying.

Translated from the Odia story 'Kanduri,' published in *Navi Samudra*, Agraduta, Cuttack, 1982.

slightest inconvenience: that seemed to be the sole purpose behind her existence. Never, not for a moment, had I seen the innocent smile of childhood flit across her lips. She never stopped crying. When she had launched a flood of tears, she would devote all her energies to ensuring that it never abated. That was why Jeje, our grandfather, had named her 'Kaanduri.' Even when she was older, no one ever thought of finding another name for her; it wasn't necessary. Although I had an elder brother's normal desire to hold the baby in my arms, my brotherly instincts had to be suppressed on account of her constant crying. She didn't just cry; she strewed the shreds of her anguish all around her. Crying was the incurable affliction she had been born with—the demon whose burden she would always carry on her shoulders. She must have started her crying while she was still in Bou's womb.

No one in the house could tolerate Kaanduri's crying. Everyone showed irritation—except Bou, that is. Her cries must have pierced Bou's skin like a vulture's sharp beak, but she never showed the pain. I always saw the same unaffected maternal face, the same acceptance, the same steadfast rhythm in her movements. Never a moan or sigh. Kaanduri's ceaseless crying made not the slightest difference to her.

When Kaanduri was only seven months old, the doctors informed us that she would never be able to speak or hear. A few months later, we were told that she would never walk. Normal above the waist, she had a pair of needle-like appendages for legs, which refused to grow. She would roll her head this way and that all day. Rolling her head around and crying to a frenzied rhythm were her only two occupations. Whenever my father looked at her, his face would shrivel up. Tendrils of helplessness clutched at the father's heart. He never reached out to hold the child in his arms. He had unconsciously accepted defeat after her birth. The storm of Kaanduri's crying had blown away every shred of affection for her.

No one in our house ever held Kaanduri in their lap. She was just ignored. Bou alone looked after her. When Kaanduri was four, Father had a rocking chair made for her at Bou's request. Kaanduri spent all her time in that chair, rocking herself, except for those moments when she was being bathed or was asleep. When she felt any discomfort—for example, when she was hungry or had soiled herself—she would make her need known by going immediately into a paroxysm of howling. If no one attended to her, she would

FIGURE 6. CRYING WAS THE INCURABLE AFFLICTION SHE HAD BEEN BORN WITH.

bite her own fingers until they bled or pull out her own hair by the roots. Bou was, therefore, always by her side.

When I think of the suffering that Bou had to go through because of Kaanduri's self-destructive behaviour, my heart sinks. Could there ever be any happiness at all in her life, I wondered? But her love for Kaanduri never wavered: she never lost her calm, never complained. Sometimes, when she was alone, she would weep quietly. She blamed herself, blamed her motherhood, her own womb. I turned bitter whenever I looked at Kaanduri. Why didn't the wretched creature die? She was not only killing herself with her crying but was bringing slow death to others. Bou was wasting her life on a living corpse.

Bou created a distance between Kaanduri and herself on one side, and the rest of us on the other, when she sensed the resentment in us. I felt Kaanduri had snatched her away, not just from me but from everyone. Bou used to visit her parents once a year, but not any more. 'I can't take Kaanduri with me and I can't leave her behind,' she would tell her brother when he wrote to her asking her to come. Kaanduri had pegged her down firmly.

The only food that Kaanduri lived on was milk. She couldn't eat with her own hands; she had to be fed. She became allergic to any other food. When she was about eight years old, she was consuming about four litres of milk a day. Fortunately, we had cows at home, so there was no problem. But that year, for some unknown reason, all the cows dried up. Milk had to be bought for Kaanduri. It was difficult for a lower-middle-class family such as ours to afford four to five litres of milk a day. One day my father was forced to tell Bou, 'Why not give Kaanduri some rice *paayas* instead of milk? We should wean her away from milk slowly.' Bou was deeply hurt. Through her tears she said, 'How much you must be spending on this, that and the other! Poor Kaanduri has a curse on her head. If she had been a normal child, wouldn't you be spending on her toys, clothes, education and what not? But because she is lying there helpless, even her food is an eyesore! The fault is mine, not hers, that I gave birth to her! I should have died before that! I beg you, please don't ever say such things again!"

What a ring of security Bou had built around Kaanduri!

I was standing next to Bou while she spoke to Father. Her words filled me with pain: I felt every drop of blood in my body had been replaced with her tears. What a mother she was! I could only pray that she should be my mother in every birth, that every unfortunate child such as Kaanduri should have such a mother! I remember reading somewhere, 'God created mothers when He realised He could not be present everywhere all the time.'

My father never said another word about Kaanduri's milk after that incident.

Kaanduri was growing in age but not in body or mind. Had she conquered age? She remained glued to that rocking chair, like a worm-eaten fruit, until the age of fourteen or fifteen. But she occupied the key position in the fortunes of our family, proclaiming the dominance of tragedy in life's drama.

When she was fifteen, the bones in her body started to melt away. She was being hollowed out. Had God decided to deny even that worm-eaten, misfortune-ridden existence? She shrank into a lump of flesh. The nightmare of death hung over her—not the rising tide of youth which is granted to others at that age. Every one of us was affected. She became more loathsome every day. Unknowingly, every one of us must have prayed for her death: we were waiting for the inevitable to happen.

But not Bou. She was expecting a miracle every day. For her, this was only a passing sickness that Kaanduri was going through. 'God, heal my Kaanduri!' she prayed as she bowed to the family deities morning, noon and evening. The daily dose of medicine, poured into Kaanduri's mouth, was never stopped. Her confidence was unshakeable.

Kaanduri's body shrank, but not the intensity of her crying. In fact, it had become much more penetrating. Even Bou would sometimes say in exasperation, 'You will be the end of me! Your crying is stripping the flesh off my bones! When will God listen to my prayers and carry me away?' I knew Bou's weariness was only of the body, not the spirit, because on some days she would hug Kaanduri close to her breast as she put kajal in her eyes and say, 'How pretty my baby is!'

That year I had joined the college near our village as a lecturer. I had to leave home at 9.00 in the morning, and returned only after 5.00. One evening, just as I was returning, I heard Bou's heart-rending cry. It seemed to have been ripped out of the core of her lacerated being. I did not know what to do. The truth of Kaanduri's end had deadened our sensibilities to such an extent that I was unprepared for this expression of grief. Kaanduri was dead. The cries of mourning were weakening.

Bou lay flattened on that lump of flesh, giving vent to one long, unending sob. 'My treasure, my hoard of gold! How I had guarded you! How could you leave me behind and run way alone? A curse on my motherhood!'

Bou still had tears to spare after all those years of grief! She was blaming herself because she had failed to keep Kaanduri alive. As though she had never dreamt that Kaanduri was going to die! Weeping as though she had lost a robust young son!

Her tears were cleansing me.

13. Rebati*

Everyone in Patpur village knew Shyam Bandhu Mohanty's home had been wiped out. Nothing remained. In just two years, the ruins had been overgrown with wild grass.

It was all Death's handiwork.

Though sending girls to school was taboo, Rebati, Shyam Babu's only daughter, went. This was more than the gods could tolerate. Within a couple of years, death—like the old woman who scours her own backyard with a basket under one arm, carefully gathering up every blade of grass—carried her father away; the next year, her mother went to the fields to relieve herself and never came back; a few months later, Basudeb, who had been tutoring Rebati, was taken away, just when the two were beginning to grow close. Only Rebati and her old grandmother remained. The old woman was convinced that Rebati's going to school was responsible for every mishap: her son and daughter-in-law had died, the farmhand had left them and the *zamindar's* men had led their bullock away. The old lady showered the choicest of curses on Rebati: 'Oh Rebati! Rebi, I say! You worthless lump of ashes from the oven!'

The news of Basudeb's death brought on a severe fever and after shivering for a couple of days Rebati grew still. The old woman thought she was no more. The jolt was enough to pull her down.

At precisely this point, Fakirmohan Senapati brings his tale 'Rebati' to a close. He writes, 'No one in the world saw any member of Shyam Bandhu Mohanty's family alive again.'

* *Rebati* is the eponymous character of a story by Fakirmohan Senapati, the father of Odia fiction, narrating the tragic life story of a young girl. The present story provides an alternative narrative.

Translated from the Odia story 'Rebati,' published in *Taraluthiba Samaya*, Bharata Bharati, Cuttack, 2010.

But here the 'world' consisted only of Patpur village in the district of Hariharpur. What the people of the village cannot see, they assume to be non-existent. Thus it is in Senapati's tale too.

She felt she was losing consciousness again. There was an unbearable pain in her chest. She didn't have the strength to open her mouth and shout. What was she to do? She got up and went inside the house. Her mouth was as dry as dust. She wasn't hungry at all, but as she groped her way in the dark she stumbled against a clay pot and knocked it over. There was a little water inside, left over from God knows when. Rebati raised the pot and gulped the water down. Then, supporting herself against the wall, she walked to the front verandah. She could see everything dimly in the darkness—the plantain trees, the guava tree, the well in the courtyard. She tried to lift her grandmother but wasn't strong enough. With great difficulty she made the old woman sit up against a stone stair leading up to the verandah, fetched some rags from inside the house and covered her up. Turning to face the house, she remembered her dead parents reverentially, touched her head to the ground and remained bowed for some time. Then she walked out boldly into the paddy fields, tottering a little—thirteen-year old Rebati, as fearless as a warrior, walking alone into the darkness of the night. She didn't know where she was going. A wisp of cotton carried by the wind...

When she awoke she found herself inside a hut. Someone had laid her down on the bed.

There was bright sunshine outside. Groaning, she tried to get up. Just then the door opened and a middle-aged man walked in, followed by a dog whose tail was wagging continuously. Seeing Rebati's attempts to get up the man cried, 'No, no, don't try to get up; there's no strength in your body. You are scratched and bruised all over.' Then he shouted to his wife, 'Gurei, come at once! The girl is awake! Bring her a little hot gruel.'

The man looked uncouth and rough. His dhoti was tucked in tightly between his legs. Dark as pitch, with curly hair and a thick moustache and a half-smoked *bidi* parked above one ear. The woman who had brought her gruel looked equally weird. But how tenderly she fed her! 'Go to sleep, child! You can get up when you feel better,' she said.

Bhobni Nahak, being of low caste, lived at one end of the village, on the edge of the jungle. His job was to guard the zamindar's barn where the grain was stored. He survived on his meagre wages, and

FIGURE 7. EACH WORD FROM REBATI IS AS SOOTHING AS SANDALWOOD PASTE TO BHOBNI AND GUREI.

Gurei, his wife, roamed through the fields around the zamindar's ponds, searching for berries, edible leaves and the occasional *chenga* fish to supplement their diet. Children they had none; there was only the dog for company. She fondly called him 'Andharia' (The Dark One).

Who could tell how far Mahajanpur was from Patpur? But that night Rebati had walked the entire distance in the darkness and fallen unconscious in the *kia* thicket beyond Mahajanpur, close to Bhobni Nahak's backyard. It was early morning and Bhobni was going out to answer nature's call. He stopped when he saw Rebati lying unconscious, as though dead. How could she have got there? At first he thought she had been the victim of some terrible crime but when he came closer he found she was alive. She must be from a good family; she was pretty and fair.

He picked her up and carried her home. When Gurei saw the child she said, 'Ma Mangala has left this child in our backyard.

When people are childless, the goddess brings them a grown child. We are the lowest of the low; who would have given us a child? But Ma Mangala has sent her to us.' Bhobni heard what she was saying and shouted, 'Stop chattering! Can't you see she is from a good family? Someone must have tried to kidnap her and dropped her here when people saw him. The poor child is unconscious. Give her some water to drink; when she is conscious she can tell us how she got here.'

They shook her and called out, still she remained in a faint, but after a long time, she got up of her own accord. Bhobni and Gurei were waiting patiently.

Rebati was unable to sleep after she regained consciousness. She had the gruel, then asked for some water and drank it. She wondered what would happen to her now. These must be good people, she thought; poor they obviously were, but only kind-hearted folk would do what they had done for her. Surely they would want to know now who she was. If they found out she was from the house of the Mohantys, would they be afraid to give her shelter? Would they take her back to Patpur? But what would she do there if she returned? Who was there to look after her?

A week passed. Rebati made an excellent recovery. Gurei followed her everywhere: 'Eat this, my child'; 'Lie down, you must be tired'; 'Come, let me comb your hair' ... She was more caring than her own mother could have been. Bhobni came to the room three times every day to find out how she was. At first he had planned to let everyone know about the child he had found and try to reunite her with her parents. But these seven days had changed his mind.

One evening, Gurei was cooking some rice in the kitchen while Rebati stood near the door. Bhobni asked the girl, with some hesitation, 'Ma, are you feeling stronger now?' Rebati nodded.

'What's your name, Ma?' he asked again.

'Rebati.'

'Where is your home?'

No answer.

'What caste are you?'

No answer.

'What's your father's name?'

No answer.

'How did you come here?'

No answer.

'Did someone bring you here or did you come yourself?'

No answer.

What more could he have asked? Suddenly Rebati began to cry. Gurei got up and rushed to her side. Bhobni became silent.

He made one more attempt to question the child but it went exactly like the last one. Now Gurei shouted at him,'Why are you troubling the girl? What can she tell you—she doesn't remember anything. Ma Mangala has sent her to us. What will you gain by stirring up her past? If her parents come looking for her, she'll go with them. But why trouble her now? She has Ma's blessing, or would she have survived? She's *our* daughter—the goddess Lakshmi herself come to our door!'

The next day, Bhobni came running with a *seula* fish in his hands. 'Do you know, Gurei,' he panted, 'the zamindar suddenly sent for me today. I was so frightened my heart went *dhaad*, *dhaad*! Had I made some mistake? Had he found out about the girl? I called on Ma Mangla for help and went to see him. "Bhobni!" the master said, "You have served me faithfully for many years, and you needn't go on living in that wilderness any longer. You will work in my *kacheri* now and your salary is raised by two rupees every month." I tell you, Gurei, I couldn't trust my own ears! I stood there, rooted to the ground, until the master said, "Why are you here still? Go home!" I've come running to tell you!'

Gurei was overjoyed. 'But where did you get the fish?' she asked.

'That's another story!' Bhobni said, squatting on the ground. 'I was walking along the bank of the pond when I heard something rustling among the weeds. I flung my *gamuchcha* into the water and threw myself down on top of it—and there was this fish! Take it and cook something for us; we will all eat together!'

As Gurei listened to Bhobni's story her eyes filled with tears, which she wiped away with the end of her sari. 'Glory be to Ma Mangala,' she said in a quivering voice. 'What is this but the work of the goddess? The child no sooner sets foot in our house than you prosper in your work. She is Lakshmi herself! And who do you think brought this fish to you?'

Rebati, inside the house, overheard everything. Tears were streaming from her eyes. The memories of Patpur, of her parents, her grandmother, Basudeb, gnawed at her heart. But what could she do? Were there any hopes to drive her footsteps forward? But she could sense already the first tender sprouts appearing, like tiny ripples forming in the stagnant waters of her mind. Her hands were sweating. Images from the past flickered and vanished—no, not images; each one was a book, a whole volume, spelling out a familiar tale.

She was thinking, with her eyes shut. What should she do? Tell Bhobni who she was? How would they react? Would they keep her if they found out she was of a high caste? Suddenly she remembered something that her Basu Bhai—Basudeb—had told her. 'Never be afraid of dangers, Rebati,' he had said. 'Whenever a danger appears, a new path will open up for you unexpectedly. You only have to recognise it.' All night she lay churned by her own thoughts and at the crack of dawn she sat up. She came out into the verandah, looked around restlessly; then, picking up a small pebble, she scratched some letters on the wall. 'Rebati Nahak.'

When Bhobni started out for the zamindar's house, whom should he find confronting him on the front verandah but Rebati? Wrapping the end of her sari round her head to show respect, she prostrated herself on the ground before him. Then she walked to the place where Gurei stood and held her in a tight embrace. And from that day, Bhobni and Gurei were her parents.

It is rumoured that on every *haat* day, Bhobni goes to the village haat and buys a couple of books which Rebati has asked for. He also buys paper, notebooks, pen and pencil. Rebati spends the entire day writing something—God knows what ! At night, she lights a *dhibiri* and sits down to read her books. She sings something in an unsteady voice. Gurei can hear her as she ignites the stove in her kitchen. Bhobni sits at the doorway, gazing fixedly at Rebati, fascinated. After the day's hard work in the zamindar's kacheri, each word from Rebati is as soothing as sandalwood paste on the skin. Bhobni and Gurei look at each other in supreme contentment.

Rebati goes on writing and reading from her books.

She was growing up.

The Nahak family did not know how to conceal their happiness.

And one evening Bhobni said to Gurei, 'Do you know, Gurei, a famous astrologer came to the zamindar's kacheri today. He looked at me and said, "Show me your right palm!" Then, looking at my palm, he said, "Lucky man!" Now I know it is my fate that has brought Rebati to us. God knows how long she will be with us!'

14. Responsibility

It was only of Gurupada that I could think; nothing else in the newspaper was of any interest. That lean, bearded face which I had known during my student days kept returning—the sharp, melancholy features, those piercing eyes...

Had he been forced to make a retreat then?

The sun was about to set; the day's business was almost over. I could imagine him in the gathering darkness, lying on a bare rope-knit cot in the courtyard of a thatched hut in a small village.

I had met him only a month ago. He had put on some flesh and the beard was missing. He looked cheerful. He gave me a big hug as soon as he saw me, but I hadn't recognised him, even when we were face to face. How could I? He had changed so much! We were meeting after almost eleven years, not just a year or two. But he said I looked just the same.

We had both joined S. C. S. College, Puri, after matriculating and shared a room in the hostel. Neither knew anything about the other. I was from a village near Puri and he from Pattamundei, in Cuttack; my clothes were almost new, his in tatters; my bed was always tidy; his, invariably messy. I was fair-skinned; he, dark. I wore covered shoes; he, Hawaiian slippers, which he dragged all the way from the lavatory to the college. He was reserved and mostly silent, while I loved to talk. My handwriting was practically illegible while his was exquisite, the letters small and rounded like brinjal seeds. His marks in the matriculation examination were much higher than mine. I hadn't been able to learn even the 'S' of 'Sanskrit,' whereas he could, when required, quote freely from the Gita and the Upanishads.

Translated from the Odia story 'Dayitwa,' published in *Dena*, Vidyapuri, Cuttack, 1998.

Despite these differences, we became the closest of friends. My worst quality was my lack of patience; Gurupada, on the other hand, faced even the most difficult situation calmly and uncomplainingly. His tolerance and ability to carry others along with him made him fit to be a 'guru.' He was in the habit of studying late into the night before an examination, keeping the light on, while I couldn't sleep if there was a light in the room; so he moved out with his books and notebooks to the verandah in front, where the light was on all night.

The closer I came to Gurupada the more aware I became of my inferiority. But he always said he was unable to achieve what he wanted. I came to know that his father was an ordinary peasant. He had to give out most of his land to sharecroppers as he suffered from asthma. Gurupada had four sisters and a brother, Umapada, who was the youngest in the family; Gurupada was the eldest.

He wanted to become a teacher in the village school after he graduated. The Secretary of the school had promised him a job. Whenever he talked of his home and his family he would become tearful. 'All the family responsibilities are on my shoulders,' he would say. 'My father is an invalid and my mother is incapable of managing anything. I have to look after the lands, take care of my sisters and brother...' I have never seen so young a person so conscious of his responsibilities.

From time to time there was a letter from someone at home and Gurupada would rush off hurriedly, with his brown *jhola* hanging from one shoulder. When he returned, a day or two later, he looked exhausted. Within those first two years in the college, one of his sisters was married and his father passed away. Then, he had to sell off a piece of land to finance another sister's marriage. He said if he had to sell any more of the land his family would starve.

It was the last year of our BA course. Gurupada had given up the room in the hostel and found cheaper lodging elsewhere; he had also taken up a couple of tuitions to manage his expenses. Nevertheless, he passed the History Honours course with Distinction. I didn't meet him for a long time after we graduated. He had already grown a beard then. When I met him in Cuttack, three years later, he hadn't changed. He told me he was teaching in the village school and had got married. I gave him the most recent information about myself: I had got into the State Civil Service but hadn't thought about marriage yet. That was to be our last meeting for a long time and he looked just as sickly as he had during that first year in college, although his beard was thicker.

And this was why I had failed to recognise him immediately when we met on the street recently. In the course of our conversation I asked him about his family. My question seemed to stir him into new life. He said happily, 'They are all well, brother. I am free of my responsibilities at last. My sisters are happily married; Umapada is the Labour Welfare Officer at Sambalpur. He was married three years ago and has a beautiful little daughter. A second child was born recently and I had gone to Sambalpur for the *ekoisia*. I am only just returning. What luck—our meeting here so unexpectedly!'

I hadn't seen him for eleven years. But the Gurupada I had known all along was a very different person now. It was as if he had only just been released from a cage in which he had been imprisoned. His wings were fluttering impatiently; he had found his voice. How happily he talked about himself! He said, 'I am going to appear at the MA examination as a private candidate and then do my PhD. I am really keen to study but wasn't able to, all these years, because of my responsibilities. But everything is fine now; my mother lives with Umapada and his wife and I am completely free.'

He went on chatting, and I listened, fascinated. He had never spoken about his family problems to anyone but me. None of his schoolmates from the village had made it to the college and I was perhaps his only friend from the student days. He just couldn't stop talking about the past, dwelling on each detail: how he had had to mortgage his lands and was able, eventually, to recover them. How he had resolved not to raise a family of his own until all his sisters had been married. Many such things.

The substance of it all was that now he was free, free. I was so happy for him. My friend had started to live only now, after years of mortification. He could have his own life. A daughter had been born and a second child was expected. There was flesh at last on that skeletal face. It was so reassuring!

But now everything has gone topsy-turvy once again. The bony face is back. I can see Gurupada sitting in the unpaved courtyard of his home, with his head drooping. Brooding.

I looked at the newspaper again. 'Fatal road accident.'

> Sambalpur, 22 August. In a tragic accident which occurred at 8.00 p.m. yesterday at the junction of the local Gole Bazaar, the Labour Welfare Officer, Sri Umapada Das, lost his life. His scooter was completely

> smashed in a head-on collision with a motor car. Investigation reveals that Sri Das hailed from Belpada village in Pattamundei, Cuttack. He was only 25 at the time of the accident and is survived by his widow, aged 21, his old mother and two daughters. The older child is one and a half years old and the younger only 2 months old. Sri Das was a very popular officer—soft-spoken, friendly and helpful. His untimely death has come as a blow to the people of this area.

I had read many reports of road accidents earlier but this was different. It raised a sudden storm of apprehension within me. The casualty was not Umapada but Gurupada. It was his life that had been snuffed out.

I heard someone say, 'Now that I have no responsibilities, I can resume my studies. I will do my MA privately and then my PhD.'

15. Sukanti's House

Sukanti's letter stirred up a swarm of memories.

Who writes letters in this Internet age? Yet Sukanti had written her a letter which was like a warm hug. Ah, Sukanti!

Pratima hadn't given anyone her address as they had just moved to Bhubaneswar. Then how did Sukanti get her address?

Sukanti and she had been classmates at both school and college and even shared a room in the hostel. The glue of friendship endured and the relationship continued. Letters were frequently exchanged but they had lost contact during the last fourteen or fifteen years—except for a five-minute meeting on the platform at Balasore station. Pratima was travelling to Calcutta and Sukanti to Berhampur. Pratima's train arrived first and, like the villain in a Hindi movie, broke up the reunion; the two friends didn't even have time to introduce their husbands to each other.

And now Sukanti had written her a letter.

That day, Pratima had failed to recognise her old friend. Sukanti had lost weight and grown darker. The two front teeth had begun to protrude. Holding her in a tight embrace, Pratima said, 'Aren't you well, Sukanti? You look terrible!'

Sukanti's familiar child-like laughter rang out. 'Oh, there's nothing the matter with my health,' she said. 'But we are building a new house in Bhubaneswar and what you see is the result of that. My husband has no time at all; he will pay the bills but that's all. Who is going to run after the labourers and masons? I have to do everything.'

Sukanti's husband was a bank officer who had risen from the ranks. Although Sukanti didn't look too well, her eyes still sparkled

Translated from the Odia story 'Sukantira Ghara,' published in *Taraluthiba Samaya*, Bharata Bharati, Cuttack, 2010.

when she talked though her tongue moved much faster than before. After she mentioned the house they were building, she had filled in a wealth of detail, all within five minutes—so much so that Pratima could learn nothing new about her husband and children.

FIGURE 8. SUKANTI RUSHED INTO HER BEDROOM AND CAME BACK WITH AN ALBUM OF PHOTOGRAPHS.

Giving Pratima's shoulder a shake, Sukanti said, 'You know, Pratima, we had the plans for our house drawn up by a famous architect. You must have heard his name?' Pratima did not reply for she had not heard the name of *any* architect. Her husband was a college professor and they had one son. He wanted to move to the village after retirement and whenever there was talk of building a house in Bhubaneswar he would say, 'I can't even look after our ancestral house in the village; what will I do with another house?'

To change the subject, Pratima had told Sukanti, 'We are going to Calcutta for a couple of days. He has a seminar and I am tagging along. The Kali temple in Belur is too much of a temptation.' As Sukanti said nothing about Berhampur, Pratima asked no questions. Sukanti returned to the first paragraph of her narrative about the house. Her husband and a colleague would soon visit Rajasthan in quest of marble for the flooring. The brass fittings were coming from

Calcutta. The house had risen to lintel level. She herself oversaw the mixing of sand and cement, standing in the sun all day.

Pratima's train arrived just then but Sukanti's narrative continued. Hurriedly she said, 'You know, the price of steel is rising but my husband insists nothing but Tiscon rods must be used in the new house.'

That was the last line. Then the two friends were separated. When Pratima's train drew away, Sukanti was scampering along the platform in search of her husband.

Pratima kept thinking about her. She hadn't been put off by Sukanti's garrulousness at all; on the contrary, she experienced a feeling of warmth for her talkative childhood friend. There were some who called Sukanti foolish, but Pratima found her simple-hearted. So simple that she could be an enigma sometimes. How excited she was just because she was building a house!

And now the unexpected letter. She needed a tool to open the envelope with and raised her hand to her head to pull out a hair-clip. At once she was reminded of an incident that had taken place when she was in the seventh class at school.

It was a pair of hair-clips that had brought her close to Sukanti. Five girls, all from villages in the vicinity, all new to the school, shared a room in the hostel. Pratima's mother had bought the hair-clips for her. One day she found them missing from the bookshelf where she had put them. She looked everywhere, asked everyone. Sukanti wasn't in the room at the time. Later, during school prayers, she saw the clips displayed proudly in Sukanti's hair. She felt so angry that she wanted to pull them out at once, but managed to retain her calm and merely said, 'Those clips are mine. Where did you find them?'

Surprisingly, Sukanti wasn't perturbed at all. She merely laughed and said 'My mother sent them to me yesterday. Do you like them? Here, take them!' She pulled them out of her hair and offered them to Pratima.

How shameless can one get, Pratima thought. Offering me my own clips after stealing them! Anyway, we have to share a room for a whole year at least and there's no point in starting a quarrel. She was unable to speak to Sukanti but the other girl's behaviour wasn't affected in any way.

Two days later, she found her missing hair-clips among the pages of a thick dictionary. Her head was in a whirl. So Sukanti had spoken the truth! 'How wrong of me to suspect her!' she rued. One could only admire her generosity in offering her own clips to Pratima.

She had apologised profusely but Sukanti laughed the incident away, and after that day the two became the closest of friends.

Pratima opened the envelope and read Sukanti's letter more than once. How many things had she written about! Her two daughters; her in-laws; the village where they lived. The death of her parents. The apathy of her two brothers. The sale of their share of the family property, and lastly, the new house in Bhubaneswar.

> Pratima, we have spent more than thirty lakhs on the house, [Sukanti had written] and are drowning in debt. But the good thing is, everyone who takes a look at the house says there's nothing to compare with it in the neighbourhood! You *must* come and see us. I am sending you our address. My two daughters are dying to see you. It was stupid of me not to have asked you for your telephone number that day at Balasore. I could have contacted you easily. Anyway, do come. My husband is still at Berhampur, but he comes here every weekend. You'll come, won't you—promise? After all, you are living in Bhubaneswar.
>
> Yours,
>
> Sukanti

Her letter was identical in style to the way she talked. Pratima could almost feel her presence. She decided that she and her husband would visit Sukanti that very day, after he returned from college.

Sukanti was living in Kanan Vihar—fifteen kilometres from Pratima's rented house in Old Bhubaneswar. On top of it, the unceasing September rains! As soon as Pratima's husband arrived, she announced—dinner had already been cooked and Kuber, the auto-rickshaw driver, summoned. Half an hour to get there, another half-hour to return and half an hour at Sukanti's. If they left early they could be back before nine.

The professor was offered no choice. The auto-rickshaw spluttered off at precisely ten past seven.

How splendid Sukanti's house must be, Pratima was thinking. Today, she would only have a first look. On her next visit she would spend half a day there and make a thorough survey. 'Wait until you see what a house my friend has built. You will be left wide-eyed!' she told her husband.

It took much more than half an hour to get there. They went past the petrol pump next to the police station, past the dairy and reached Plot No. 387 at last. But what was the babu's name, the neighbours wanted to know. It must be on the nameplate, she retorted.

Hearing the commotion, Sukanti stepped out onto the verandah. She reached out through the grill door and switched on the light outside. She was followed by her two daughters, both of whom were studying in a local engineering college. There was much happiness and laughter! The two friends were locked in a tight embrace. Pratima's husband was greeted with an effusive namaskar.

Now they all walked into the house. Two bedrooms, a drawing room, a dining area and kitchen. A very ordinary house. There were a thousand questions in Pratima's mind. Sukanti had written that the house was complete and had cost thirty lakhs and was the most spectacular house in the neighbourhood. But *this*? Surely, Sukanti would never lie!

Tea, biscuits and other snacks were served. Sukanti couldn't restrain her laughter as she talked.

Pratima could not wait any longer. She asked directly, 'You wrote the house cost thirty lakhs. Is this it?'

There were peals of laughter from Sukanti. She said, 'Why on earth should I be living in *that* house? Our house is in Jagannath Vihar, near Siripur. Didn't I tell you—the loan with interest looked about to swamp us! The two girls are going to the engineering college, just five minutes away. The loan will take years to pay off, and he will have retired by then. We have rented the house to a multinational company. Wait, I'll show you the photographs.'

Having said all this in a single breath, Sukanti rushed into her bedroom and came back with an album of photographs. She took them through the photographs, one after the other, with great pride. The same laughter, the same carefree talk. The same sparkle in the eyes.

Returning home in the auto-rickshaw, Pratima tried to recall what the house had looked like. But she could remember nothing at all.

16. The Bicycle

Tuna said, 'Grandfather, your poetry is just like your old bicycle.'

Sudhir Babu looked at his grandson leafing through a magazine. He was in the seventh class and in his thirteenth year, but his critical sense was remarkable. Sudhir Babu said, just to annoy the lad, 'Why, do you hear my poetry creaking? Or its bell tinkling?'

The grandson was not to be put off. 'No, Grandfather, I don't hear any such sounds. But your poems are as old-fashioned as your bicycle. Write poetry by all means if you have to, but must you go on repeating "bicycle, bicycle" all the time? "The bicycle is my friend," "The bicycle is my life," "The bicycle is my body," and so on. A lot of rubbish, if you ask me! It's high time you got rid of that bicycle. It's nothing but garbage, littering up the house!'

Having said this, the boy flung the magazine down on the bed and walked off.

Sudhir Babu was speechless for a minute. '"Old fashioned garbage," he says!' he muttered.

For the last two years, that bicycle had been the theme of all his poems. They had been published in various magazines, and readers had written letters praising them. A publisher had even offered to put them together in a collection. But his grandson declared it was rubbish!

Well, well—what can the child know of poetry? Can symbolism mean anything to him? Then why take his criticism to heart? At first, Sudhir Babu had treated the affair lightly, but that evening, when he picked up his pen to write yet another poem on the same theme, his hand jerked to a stop. The old bicycle suddenly seemed to confront him—thickly coated with dust, paint peeling off from

Translated from the Odia story 'Cycle,' published in *Taraluthiba Samaya*, Bharata Bharati, Cuttack, 2010.

the rusted frame, mudguards bent and battered, the seat pointing backwards. The object that had inspired a hundred poems stood before him, accusing him.

He hadn't ridden the bicycle for at least five years. But that did not mean that he had distanced himself from it. They might have been separated physically, but it still filled every fragment of his consciousness.

FIGURE 9. SUDHIR BABU AND RAJANI ON VEERSEN.

He felt he had to get up and take a look at the bicycle at once.

It had been standing in the same position, leaning against the wall in a corner of the front verandah, for the last five years. He opened the front door and stepped out into the verandah. The bicycle was almost hidden behind a shroud of dust, grime and cobwebs. The tyres were deflated, robbed of their life-breath; the seat was about to fall off; the mudguards were dented in a dozen places. All traces of paint had vanished long ago. He gazed and gazed.

Yes, it was true. He hadn't touched the bicycle once during the two years which he had spent writing poetry dedicated to it. Not one loving touch, not one whisper of commiseration. Well, he might not have ridden it, but shouldn't he have taken some care of it? What would it have said to him if it could speak? What a burden of hurt feelings it must be carrying!

Memories returned. The bicycle had entered his life forty-five years ago, at the same time as Rajani. She was a new bride then and it had been a brand new, green 'Made in England' Humber with twin forks. With a German bell on the handlebar, the sound of which could be heard across the neighbourhood. Fitted with a Lucas dynamo whose majestic hum filled the air when he pedalled along a lonely road. The powerful beam from the lamp lit up the night.

Once, several of his friends and he had gone on a picnic. Everything was loaded onto five bicycles, carrying eight grown men between them. The picnic spot was seven to eight kilometres away from the village. They had taken a Petromax to provide light. Food was cooked; the fun and frolic paused. They sat down to eat in the purple glow of sunset. It soon grew dark, but when they tried to light the Petromax, it only spluttered and coughed. What were they to do? They were in the middle of a forest; it was necessary to get back soon. Then someone had a brainwave. 'I say, Sudhir's bicycle has a dynamo, doesn't it? It's more powerful than any Petromax.' The cycle was put on its stand and they took turns to turn the crank, making the rear wheel go round, while the rest sat down to eat. When it was time to return, Sudhir Babu's bicycle led the way. No other bicycle had a dynamo. So it was that the bicycle came to the rescue.

It had borne the burden of Sudhir Babu, his son, daughter and countless friends patiently through the years. Innumerable bags filled with vegetables had been slung from its handlebars; also sometimes fish and sometimes meat. Goods ordered by Rajani had been carried home on it from the market. She never visited the market—it wasn't done in her family, she said. So, on *Rajo*, *Savitri amavasya*, *Holi* or other festivals, Sudhir Babu had to fetch eight or ten saris for her approval from a known shopkeeper and she would select one; the others were returned. It was the bicycle that had to do all the fetching and returning. True, Sudhir Babu pedalled, but whose was the labour?

Sudhir Babu often felt the bicycle was alive to all that was going on. That was why, on his way to the college, he frequently entered into conversation with it. 'You know, friend,' he would begin, 'Rajani has become rather irritable these days. I don't like it at all. She has sat on your front rod a couple of times, hasn't she? How shy she used to be! And now she gets upset so easily! I wonder what's wrong. You remember those days in Sundargarh, don't you? Our son was about to be born. He was expected on the twenty-eighth but the labour pains began on the twelfth. How she suffered! It was night and there was not a rickshaw to be found. The hospital didn't have an ambulance. You seemed to be telling me something in gestures only I saw. So I spread out a bed-sheet across your front rod and lifted Rajani onto it. Remember that freezing winter night? How many minutes did it take us to reach the hospital? And those two nurses—they were the Mother incarnate! God knows what they did, but the child was born almost immediately.

'That son has married and become a father now. That rascal of a grandson is in the seventh class, and a new bicycle, fitted with shock absorbers, has been bought for him. Bright red in colour. Why should he even glance at you? Old-fashioned garbage, he calls you.'

He was turning over page after page from the scrapbook of memories. In all these episodes, he had been a participant—but the real hero was the bicycle.

In an emotional moment he had given it a name—Veersen. Raja Prithviraj Chauhan's horse was called Chetak and Alexander the Great had named his horse Bucephalus. Then why shouldn't the 'Made in England' green Humber have a name? Sometimes, when he had to clean and oil the machine, he would call out to his wife, 'Do you hear? Bring me some coconut oil mixed with a little kerosene. I have to attend to Veersen.'

He taught English in a college. His entire professional life had been spent in Veersen's company. Even after retirement, Sudhir Babu could be seen engaged in various odd jobs around the city, mounted on Veersen. His visits to the Government Treasury, library and literary meetings were all performed with Veersen's help. His friends teased him: Veersen was the elixir that helped preserve his health.

Five years ago, Sudhir Babu had ridden Veersen to a friend's home on a visit. The forty-year old bicycle and its sixty-three-year old rider usually made a safe pair; but God knows what happened that day—Sudhir Babu rode headlong into a telephone pole and had to be carried to the hospital. When he returned home, three days later, Veersen had been consigned to the position on the front verandah which it has occupied to this day.

'No more bicycle rides for you!' his son had announced. 'You were lucky to get off so lightly.'

Then Sudhir Babu remembered: his vision had suddenly blurred as he cycled along and his head had reeled. But he could not recall how he had collided with the telephone pole.

From that day, Veersen lay neglected.

His son did not attempt to sell off the old bicycle or otherwise get rid of it, out of regard for his father, but neither did he try to get it repaired. And now the grandson says, 'Throw it out; it's garbage!'

Sudhir Babu picked up a rag and wiped away some of the dust. Then he tried to take the bicycle off the verandah, onto the road outside.

His son had gone to the office and his daughter-in-law was busy in the kitchen. His grandson was studying. Rajani was in the backyard, doing something. The coast was clear. Sudhir Babu walked ahead, dragging the bicycle with one hand. 'Brother Veersen,' he said, 'you have suffered unpardonable neglect. I may not be able to ride you again, but that doesn't mean you will be left uncared for. I have been in agony ever since that grandson of mine called you garbage! Come, I'm going to get you thoroughly overhauled—whatever the cost.'

Sudhir Babu felt tired after he had dragged the old bicycle for some distance. Finally, he arrived at Banamali's Bicycle Repair Shop. Banamali was renowned for his magic touch with old bicycles. Getting the bicycle to lean against a wall, Sudhir Babu said, 'Banamali, I'm leaving my bicycle here. Repair it; do whatever is necessary—but I want it to look like new! Can you do it?' Banamali said he would need a week.

When Sudhir Babu returned seven days later, the old bicycle had been transformed. It was once again Veersen, the battle-horse!

Banamali handed over the slip of paper on which he had totalled up the costs. Sudhir Babu paid up without wasting a word. Had it been something else he would surely have bargained—but not where Veersen was involved.

Veersen came home again.

His son, shocked and incredulous, stared by turns at his father and the bicycle. Rajani came out and had a look. Sudhir Babu sat down in an armchair and regarded the bicycle with supreme satisfaction. Just then, his grandson appeared. 'Grandfather, is this your old bicycle?' he asked. 'That's wonderful! I'll have two bicycles now. I've outgrown the other one—it's too low for me.' He laughed happily.

He did not wait to hear what his grandfather would have to say. Trundling the bicycle down from the verandah, he rode off in a flash.

Sudhir Babu's mind grew bright, as though he had been revived by a breath of fresh air. He went into his room, picked up pen and paper and began to write.

A new poem was burgeoning, like the tender shoot of a plant. Sudhir Babu was sure that Tuna would like *this* poem, for like the bicycle, it would represent the new age.

17. The Noose

Sudhir Babu woke up with a start and got up, sweating profusely. He felt he had just heard a cow lowing loudly, directly behind his ear. How strange! He had never had such a weird experience before!

Several hours of the night still remained. Emptiness all around: no one in the house. Summer vacation had begun and Bilasini and his daughter had left. It was the same every year—she left for her father's home as soon as the vacation arrived and Sudhir Babu was left alone to guard the house. The college was close by but the place felt deserted. The danger of burglary always lurked. Besides, all the dreary routines of the annual examination had to be gone through—answer-books had to be marked, records filled in. The Principal frequently put Sudhir Babu in charge and summer vacation normally meant, therefore, Bilasini's annual visit to her parental home and Sudhir Babu's examination duties.

He looked at the clock on the wall: 3:40 a.m.

He increased the speed of the ceiling fan and tried to go back to sleep.

Thoughts came swarming. It was normal for him to toss restlessly in bed if, for any reason, he woke up in the middle of the night. Sleep wouldn't return easily. He had to go to the bathroom repeatedly; his eyes smarted; he would get up again and again and drink some water. He gulped down a tumblerful now and felt a little better.

He made another attempt to go to sleep.

Sleep must have overcome him at some time without his knowing it. It was then that he heard the lowing once more—much louder this time. He sat up again, as though an electric current had

Translated from the Odia story 'Phasa,' published in *Taraluthiba Samaya*, Bharata Bharati, Cuttack, 2010.

run through him. Bright sunshine already. And true enough, just outside the gate was a cow, lowing pitifully, obviously searching for its lost calf.

He looked at the cow, remembered what had happened last night and smiled. It must have been the same cow—and he had imagined it lowing close to his ear!

The day passed smoothly. His daughter Julie and Bilasini had rung from Sambalpur. They must be enjoying themselves. Bilasini always looked forward avidly to this time of the year. The annual trip to the parental home awakened, so it was said, memories of carefree maidenhood. Could she be expected to understand the pangs of loneliness that Sudhir went through as he counted out the dragging hours, minutes and seconds?

Night returned. Sudhir made chapattis, *dalma* and salad for himself and then sat down to read *Power Shift*, by his favourite author Alvin Toffler. Toffler had predicted the explosion of wealth and violence in the twenty-first century. Events would no longer be controlled by place and direction; innumerable episodes would unfold, driven by the forces of motion and inertia. His two other books, *Future Shock* and *Third Wave*, had created a revolution globally.

Sudhir was a professor of English. He was bitterly opposed to superstition, useless observance of customs in the name of tradition and uncritical reverence for the past. In his view, human beings had to be rational before they could be anything else. The future could be confronted only if such a society could be created. Every crisis could be faced through rationality and logical thinking, not through superstition.

He had barely started on *Power Shift* when he was caught up in a maelstrom of swirling thoughts. He wasn't even aware when sleep came and draped him in a veil of darkness.

Sleep was abruptly shattered, however, by the sound of lowing. He got up from bed and walked to the front door, intending to shoo away the offending cow from the gate. But there was no cow to be seen. Stillness everywhere. He came to the gate, looked around, from one end of the road to the other. No, no one there at all. But he was sure he had heard the cow. Right next to the bedroom window.

What was going on?

Could the cow have disappeared after it had lowed? In the middle of the night? He went back to bed but sleep eluded him. The remainder of the night was spent in tossing from side to side. He went from this room to that, turned over the pages of the book, but his mind remained restless.

Another morning and another night. Sudhir reconnoitered the front and back of the house thoroughly before he went to bed. If there was a cow anywhere he would chase it away—but where was the cow?

He came back to his bedroom and lay down on the bed.

A strange image flickered across his consciousness. Directly in front of him was the head and face of a cow. An innocent face. Large black pupils. Not just black—those eyes were suffused with a mysterious darkness—a darkness that stretched into unknown depths. Sudhir shivered. He focused away from the eyes and gazed at the face. What a beautiful face, so full of simplicity, and yet so sad! Hot breaths emanated from its nostrils. The smell of tender grass came from the mouth. A few strands of half-chewed grass dangled from the corners of the lips. The cow's grazing had been interrupted.

'Why, this is our Silva!' Sudir blurted out. 'Why couldn't I recognise her?' He was basking in the warmth of his own feelings now. Silva! She had been glistening white. When she stood in the sunshine after she had bathed she shone like silver. She was not plain white but a different, silvery white! And so Sudhir Mohapatra, Professor of English, had named her 'Silva.' 'Our Silva is pure silver!' he had declared happily.

Then suddenly the cow opened its mouth and let out a bellow, right in front of his eyes. He felt its hot breath on his face.

He sat up, filled with a kind of fear.

He had lived in that government bungalow for seven years. There was no danger of his being transferred again, once he had been posted to this college; and so, to meet Bilasini's demand for pure milk, he had bought a cow. A hybrid Jersey animal.

Once the cow had been tied up in front of the house they felt the need for a cowshed. Fodder had to be bought. Sudhir Babu was a man of taste. His cow had to look as sleek, as well-groomed as her master. Not only was a comfortable cowshed erected but a brush was procured, so that the cow could be tended to after her bath. She had been named 'Silva' though Bilasini had suggested, 'Let us call her "Dhobali" (the White One), so that everyone can understand,' which Sudhir Babu had turned down.

Now a lot of the professor's time was spent with Silva. He loved to play with her little calf. He talked to the animal as though he was human. He bought a necklace of beads from the market and put it around his little neck. The cowshed became the centre of his attention; before he went to bed at night, he would inspect the shed and make sure everything was all right. The cow and the calf took up so much of his time that his studies suffered, but he was enjoying the time so spent. He had no wish now to go out of the house, even for a day. If his friends called him for a picnic he would say, 'Sorry, but who will look after Silva if I am not at home?'

He cleaned out the cowshed himself, milked the cow, fed the two animals. They were living in a town, where there were no fields for Siva and the calf to graze in. Once in a while, but only when he was present, Sudhir would let the animals loose inside the compound of the house, before he tied them up himself.

Once Silva and the calf had strayed out of the gate and wandered off a little distance. Sudhir made a desperate search for them and tears had come to his eyes. Silva's beauty had captivated him; he was in love with the animal. During the summer months, when grass became scarce, he would go searching for a few blades of grass, with his gardening hoe in his hand, and feed the two animals lovingly.

And, in fact, Silva's milk was exquisitely sweet. Thick and creamy. Not once had she resisted or thrown a tantrum while she was being milked. She was the epitome of bovine virtues.

And so, when cleaning out the shed, Sudhir felt as happy as the mythical King Dilip, who had rejoiced in serving Nandini, the divine cow.

It was the same Silva who had come to startle him now. But why did she look so pitiful? And why was there such fear in his heart when he heard the animal lowing?

Silva was no more; she had passed away a year ago. Here, in this very bungalow. In the cowshed that had been turned into a garage.

Silva had yielded milk for a year and a half. Before the male calf was weaned, Sudhir sold it. 'Sell the calf,' everyone advised him, 'or he will turn into a little bull and become difficult to manage.' The calf was sold but Sudhir did not have the heart to sell its mother. But did Fate will otherwise? He remembered very clearly: that evening, he had let Silva loose inside the compound for a while and then tied the rope to the peg in a double loop so that she would not slip loose and wander away. He didn't want her to chew up the plants growing in flowerpots on the verandah. Silva had been alive and well when he had taken a last look at her before going to bed.

But next morning she lay spreadeagled on the ground. The rope that tied her to the peg had turned into a noose and strangled her. Sudhir untied the rope quickly—but it was all over.

Some said it was snakebite; someone else said Silva must have swallowed a poisonous caterpillar while grazing; others insisted it was a sudden attack of rheumatic fever. But Bilasini said Silva had slipped and lost her footing and the noose had done the rest.

Sudhir was inconsolable. For two days he did not eat. He picked up Silva's peg, her brush, her bucket and the rest of her belongings and threw them away at a distance. The cowshed was demolished and turned into a garage. In a few months, Silva was forgotten.

But why was she coming back now, and what made her bellow so furiously? Sudhir's daughter and wife were away. If Bilasini had been there he might have sought her advice. The neighbouring house too had lain vacant for several months, ever since Gunanidhi Babu retired.

Sudhir felt lost. For about five days, Silva came back to his dreams. Her lowing woke him up. Her intense black eyes frightened him.

That morning he thought he would call up Bilasini and ask her to come back. Their daughter could follow later. There were still about twenty days for the vacation to end. He was sitting in his bedroom, teacup in hand, debating whether or not to ask Bilasini to return, when he heard a muffled lowing outside the gate. He was stunned. He walked out to the front verandah.

There was someone standing outside the gate. Coming closer, he saw a man holding a wisp of straw between his teeth, sideways. He did not speak but spread out his hands to ask for alms. It was the indistinct sound of lowing through which he was soliciting alms. He looked sturdy and strong; a woman stood at a little distance.

Sudhir felt irritated at first. It was the woman who answered him when he asked what the matter was.

'Babu, we are from a neighbouring village,' she said. 'This is my husband. We are from a respectable home, Babu. Two days ago, our cow died while she was tethered to the peg—we don't know how it happened. Since she was tethered when she died, the *purohit* said we have committed the sin of *go-hatya*. It is a grave sin, Babu. To atone for this sin, my husband must go from door to door for seven days, with this piece of straw between his teeth, lowing like a cow to beg for alms. Then, we will go to Puri with whatever alms we have collected, bathe in the sea and purify ourselves, have a *darshan* of Jagannath and return to our village. Give us alms, Babu. We are supposed to visit seven houses every day, and there are stlll four more houses to go to today.'

Sudhir did not reply. One look at the man was enough to subdue him. He went inside, returned with a five-rupee note and gave it to the woman. The couple walked away.

He tried to reason with himself. If a cow died while it was tethered, was the owner to blame? What logic! How many cows were being slaughtered every day all over the world! For people in the West, especially, beef was an important food. But out here the sin of go-hatya, penance, purification, begging for alms from door to door with a piece of straw between the teeth, lowing like a dumb animal! Totally irrational! Superstition. Surrender to a stupid tradition.

That was all he could think of throughout the day. At first he thought of discussing the issue with someone; but then he thought, most people were traditional; they would come up with all kinds of irrelevant arguments. There was no point in talking to anyone. It was beyond the realm of the rational anyway.

But he couldn't sleep that night. The moment he closed his eyes, the face of Silva floated up before him. As soon as he dozed off, her lowing shook him up, and from time to time he heard the muffled rumbling of the man he had seen with the bit of straw held between his teeth. He felt greatly agitated. He wasn't able to liberate himself from his own noose. No matter how much he argued with himself, some question lingered. There was something that eluded logic—something that he could not understand or explain, though he thought he had settled all doubts long ago.

After ruminating all night, Sudhir came to a decision. Silva's death had occurred a year ago. There was no point, therefore, in his going from door to door with a piece of straw between his teeth. But he would go to Puri, bathe in the sea and have a darshan of the Lord.

When he was seated in the bus to Puri next morning, there was a tiny wisp of straw between his teeth. It was not visible from the outside but he wasn't speaking at all.

18. The Picture

The place: Gandhari Vidyapeetha. The time: 4.15 p.m — the last period in the school timetable. Great excitement among the children because they will soon be free to go home!

But the children of Class 6 look nervous and apprehensive. This is the Drawing Class—a time they normally enjoy, although not all of them like to draw. The reason is the Drawing Master himself. Gentle and soft-spoken, Maharana Sir first draws a picture on the blackboard as a model for the children to copy. If a child is unable to draw, the teacher does not lose his temper or ridicule the child but creates a comic situation in which the children and he laugh together, particularly if a child's drawing lacks meaning—for example, if the drawing of a brinjal would be unrecognisable but for the label 'brinjal' below it! In such a situation, the teacher produces, in an instant, such a realistic drawing of the object in the child's notebook that he feels rewarded. And so, even the least capable student looks forward to the Drawing Class with pleasant anticipation.

Maharana Babu had never been known to rebuke a student. If he felt particularly irritated he might tell a student, 'I'm not going to draw anything in your notebook today!' That's as far he would go. There was always a smile and a kind word on his lips. The children loved him and even though his class was generally held in the last period, it was always eagerly awaited.

But on the day in question he was on leave and so the Headmaster had asked someone else to engage the class. This was Bholanath Sir, the English teacher. As soon as the children saw him walk into the class, their hearts sank.

Translated from the Odia story 'Chitra,' published in *Chitrita Chaupasa*, Grantha Mandir, Cuttack, 1983.

That severe, unsmiling face in place of Maharana Sir's cheerful countenance. The nightmare of English grammar, instead of the relaxation of drawing. In Maharana Sir's class, your lines could be crooked, but the slightest error would not be tolerated in Bholanath Sir's class.

What if he asked you a question on grammar or translation!

Bholanath Sir, the strictest of all the teachers in the school, taught English. You could expect to have your ears pulled at any time. If he saw you loitering outside, he would scold and threaten. If you tried to shield your head or ears from chastisement, he would pinch you in the stomach, and the moment your hand moved down to rub the affected part—slap!

How heartless he was! The students lived in terror of him. And to think that this demon had been sent to keep them chained during the last hour, just when eager feet were beginning to move towards the door! Who would bear the brunt of Bholanath Sir's ire today?

But God alone knows what unknown spirit had descended on him that day! Instead of asking them questions on grammar, he said, 'This is supposed to be the Art Class, isn't it? As your Drawing teacher is on leave, I want each of you to draw something in your notebooks and show it to me.'

A wave of unexpected pleasure ran through the class.

What should he ask the children to draw? Bholanath Sir couldn't decide, even after a great deal of thought. He could not recall having ever drawn a single picture in his life. Had he drawn the pictures himself during the Drawing Class when he had been a student in school, or did he get his neighbour to draw them? He couldn't remember. It had been more than forty years ago. But he did remember that he had failed the drawing test. 'The idiot can't even draw a picture!' his father had remarked cynically. 'What kind of a student is he?'

Finally, he hit upon a subject. 'I want you to draw a picture of "Mother,"' he told the children at last.

They settled down to work enthusiastically. Fifteen minutes or so later, they walked up to the teacher's desk with the work they had done. Each one with a different picture. Some showed an expressionless face; some, a face in profile. Faces without ears, with two dots for eyes and a straight line for a mouth. A child who was unable to draw a straight line had produced a caricature of a human face, with ears that were larger than the rest of the features.

In keeping with his nature, Bholanath Sir should have scolded those children who couldn't draw acceptable pictures. But he showed no irritation that day.

He examined each drawing with great curiosity. The children showed him their drawings, one after the other, and went back to their seats. They were waiting for the bell to ring so that they could go home. Nearly all the children had shown their drawings to the teacher.

'Come on, it's almost time!' Bholanath Sir announced. 'Who is left?'

No one replied. That should mean they had all shown him their work.

Just then, the teacher's eyes fell on a child in the fourth row. He was trying to keep his face averted instead of looking up straight.

'You there in the blue checked shirt!' Bholanath Sir shouted. 'You haven't shown me your work, have you? Come here!'

The boy was trying to hide. But since he had been singled out, he had to stand up.

'Bring me your notebook!' the teacher roared again.

Who didn't fear that terrible voice and those glaring eyes? One shout was enough to make even a student of Class 11 perspire! And these were only children of insignificant Class 6.

Reluctantly, the boy in the blue checked shirt started his slow walk to the teacher's desk, notebook in hand. From a distance, Bholanath Sir could see—he didn't even have a pencil. 'Oh, so you don't have a pencil?' he fumed. 'You rascal! Come here, will you?'

All the children were squirming now. No escape for their friend! Was there anyone there who had never felt the weight of that hand?

At long last, the boy reached Bholanath Sir and at once, the teacher snatched the notebook from his hand. The boy was trembling.

There was not a single pencil mark in the notebook. The blood rose to Bholanath Sir's head. His breath came in quick gasps; the eyes turned into blazing coals. Twisting the boy's ear hard he said, 'Tell me, you rogue, why haven't you drawn anything? You've been sitting there, doing nothing, pretending you were working! How dare you disobey me!'

His hand was already raised. The boy's entire body shook in a paroxysm of fear. He was on the point of tears. In a trembling voice he said, 'I don't have a mother, Sir! She died soon after I was born. I've never seen her.'

19. The Rickshaw-wallah

The rickshaw-puller is not an individual; he represents a tribe. One who tills the land or builds homes for others is called a daily labourer, while someone who digs minerals out of the earth or uses his hands to produce things for a factory owner is known as an industrial worker. But the rickshaw-puller is neither labourer nor worker; he belongs to a unique species. Some employers provide housing for their workers and a bell or siren announces the start as well as end of their working day. Eight hours to a day. The labourer comes to work at appointed times and goes home when he has done his double-shift; but the rickshaw-puller's day has no hours. You can hear his bell tinkling on the open road at any time—night or day, summer or winter.

The rickshaw-puller is the most insecure of working men. If any feet can be found pounding through monsoon rain and slush, they are his. A dry leaf wafted at random by the wind.

Yet I had never felt sympathy for any rickshaw-wallah. Why should I? What qualities did they possess to win anyone's heart? You could see them enthroned on the passenger-seat, cross-legged, under a shady tree, smoking a bidi with supreme indifference to the world or sleeping with a gamuchha thrown across the face, deaf to calls or entreaties, no matter how urgent. In pouring rain or blistering sun, you could be in a feverish haste to reach the bus stand or railway station with your wife and children, but no matter how endearingly you addressed him, he would always quote an impossibly high fare, paying not the slightest heed to your status as a 'babu.'

Frequently, after you have reached your destination, he will ask for a fare in harsh tones that will send your head reeling. All

Translated from the Odia story 'Chhatire Chandan Katha,' published in *Taraluthiba Samaya*, Bharata Bharati, Cuttack, 2010.

pleading will be rejected with the same blanket statement: 'That's the fare and that's what you'll pay.' Sometimes his language will make your blood boil and you may feel tempted to raise your hand—but no, you are a 'bhadralok' and so you must swallow your pride and pay whatever is demanded.

And therefore, despite all the social abuse that the tribe is subjected to, I have felt not the slightest sympathy. I always thought it best to keep my distance from them. Better to walk than to bandy words with a rickshaw-wallah.

FIGURE 10. 'YOU IDIOT! CAN'T YOU SEE—THE BUS IS LEAVING?'

But that day I was compelled.

'How much?' I asked.

'Whatever you pay,' he replied. 'You are all educated babus; I am sure you will consider what the fare should be for that distance. Why should I ask?'

I looked at his face. Likes to talk; very sure of himself, quite likely. I calculated the distance from the postgraduate Hostel of the Medical College to the bus stand next to Jyoti Talkies. Four to five kilometres it would be. He *should* ask for ten rupees but I'll give him eight. Why should one pay whatever the rickshaw-wallah demands? Accordingly, I deposited my bag on the floor-board and climbed onto the seat hurriedly, having decided to pay no more than eight rupees.

I didn't suppose he would be drunk so early in the morning. His face looked clean and bright. Must have had a bath already. I have often found rickshaw-wallahs starting their day in an inebriated state, stinking of cheap liquor, dressed filthily. These rogues spend more on liquor than on food—in fact, less on food than on bidis even. You see them tottering in their seats. Someone who had made a survey of rickshaw-wallahs' slums had written,'Wife-beating is common and the main reason is drunkenness.'

I was afraid the man might be an addict, in which case my hurry to reach the bus stand would be in vain. The bus to Khandapara leaves at 6.00 a.m. sharp. It's almost 5.35 now. Only twenty-five minutes to go and it's nearly five kilometres to the bus stand. Anxiety gripped me.

I had brought my father to the hospital at Berhampur, with Lokenath Kakei (Uncle) as an escort. As a close friend of my father, he was almost a member of the family. His son Gadadhar was doing a postgraduate course at the Medical College and so we had rushed to Berhampur. My father would have to remain in the hospital for a week. Lokenath Kakei had left the day before. There was no other source of help, so I would have to rush to Khandapara for some more money and get back to Berhampur by the evening. I was camping in Gadadhar's room in the hostel.

The rickshaw had reached the Kampalli crossroads.

No, my rickshaw-wallah was perfectly sober and pedalling away at a fairly good clip. Sweat poured down his thin legs. His *ganji* was soaked.

I had told him, as soon as we crossed the hospital, 'Look, I have barely twenty minutes. If I don't reach the bus stand before six I'll be in serious trouble. Can you go fast?' And immediately, he had poured all his might into the job. But I was probably expecting the speed of a motor car. Why not—he wasn't giving me a free ride; I was paying good money, wasn't I?

Sitting on the seat behind him, I was watching him closely. Thin frame; medium-dark complexion. A torn ganji covering his bony chest. Chequered lungi, lifted above the knees and tucked into his waist. Bare feet.

They looked surprisingly clean. The heels were not cracked. Streams of sweat flowed down to his ankles. But he had not slackened pace.

Where was he from? He did not look like a Telugu-speaker. Most rickshaw-wallahs in Berhampur speak Telugu. He could be from Nayagarh—that's a place which breeds a lot of rickshaw-pullers and taxi drivers.

I looked at my watch. Eight minutes to six. The rickshaw had just crossed the Tata–Benz junction. I said, somewhat angrily, 'Are you playing games? Hurry up! I won't pay you a paisa if I miss my bus.'

He did not reply.

I could see he was trying his hardest. But I was using my words as a whip. Maybe I could make him go faster.

When we were just opposite Khallikote College, we nearly collided with another rickshaw. I shouted out, 'Are you a man or a beast? Can't you see where you're going? Do you want to kill me in your haste to earn money?'

I knew he was not to blame. A stray cow had suddenly rushed out of the stadium and he had swerved to avoid it. The other rickshaw had emerged abruptly from a side lane. He had shown great presence of mind in avoiding a collision—and here I was, screaming at the man!

Well, such outbursts are necessary from time to time to keep these rogues in line.

It was exactly 6:00 when we reached the bus stand. The Berhampur–Khandapara bus was already rolling. Another minute and it would drive away.

I was in a frenzy. There was a storm raging within. I shouted at him, 'You idiot! Can't you see—the bus is leaving?'

As if he was my bonded slave! What had prevented me from starting ten minutes earlier? I shouted at him mercilessly. But he was pedalling away for all he was worth, as though his life was at stake.

The bus conductor saw us just then. The rickshaw-wallah was imploring him to wait, with folded hands. I was desperate to jump out of the rickshaw.

The bus slowed down and came to a halt. I quickly pulled out a twenty-rupee note and said, breathlessly, 'Quick ! Give me the change. Twelve rupees!'

'Babu, where can I find the change so early in the morning?' he said.

Trying to hop onto the foot-board of the bus I said to the conductor, 'Can you give him eight rupees? I'll pay you back later.' But he said, 'There's no change.'

The bus was picking up speed. I was holding on to a door-handle, running and trying to jump on board. My bag threatened to slip off my shoulder. The twenty-rupee note was still in my hand. The rickshaw-wallah was running in step with me.

Just then he said, 'Let it be, babu! The bus is leaving; get inside! You can pay me later. Be careful, the door may crush your hand!'

Someone seemed to be pushing me from behind. I got into the bus. The conductor slammed the door shut. The bus leapt forward. The rickshaw-wallah was left behind. I had just a glimpse of his face.

The bus was moving fast now. The twenty-rupee note was still clutched in my hand. I had a hundred-rupee note in my purse, apart from the twenty-rupee note. The ticket to Khandapara would cost fifty, maybe fifty-five rupees. The man should rightfully have got ten rupees. I had said I would pay eight. He hadn't opposed me. The bus was leaving and so he had not insisted on being paid. 'Let it be, babu!' he had said. 'You get into the bus!' The money was in my hand. I could have given him the twenty-rupee note and he would owe me ten, perhaps twelve rupees. But he had shown consideration which was beyond me!

I got into a seat quietly, overwhelmed by a feeling of repentance and humiliation.

I have lost count of the number of times I have visited Berhampur after this incident. I worked in a bank there for a few months and later was a lecturer in Khallikote College for a couple of years. Whenever I walk into the street I glance at the faces of the rickshaw-wallahs, searching for a lost face. I hear the whisper in my ears, 'Payment can wait; you can pay me later. Careful now—the door is about to bang shut!'

That unpaid debt haunts me. But I look at rickshaw-wallahs differently now.